GULLY & GRACE

TOY

CHAPTER 1

race

It was opening night for my baby my new pet project. I was surprised at the turn out. I had put my blood sweat and tears into this place. To see the community, show out for me almost made me emotional. I say almost because I was raised not to show emotions. I found it funny that my mother named me Grace but, she died not long after I was born leaving me to be raised by my father. My father, Greg was a retired District Attorney for the city of Norfolk. He didn't raise me alone which is why I always dressed as a woman should. He had the help of his sister; my Auntie GiGi and three brothers, which are Geon, Gary, and Geoff whose name is pronounced Jeff. I don't know what the deal was with my grandparents and all the damn 'G' names. Even Auntie GiGi's real name is Georgette. Don't get it twisted my Auntie GiGi raised me to act and dress like a lady but, that's where the lady shit stopped. My father and uncles made sure I was up on all the games that men tried to run on women. I was trained in boxing and how to carry a gun by the time I turned sixteen. I didn't take shit from anyone maybe, that's why my ass was single as fuck right now. I wasn't lonely but, I was definitely single. Most of the men I've run across would argue that I had the mindset of a man. Maybe, I did but that wasn't going to change. It was because of those lessons that they taught me that I wasn't one of the many single women raising babies alone and waiting for a man to take care of me. I only needed a man for one thing and one thing only. Once that was done, they could go on their merry way.

"Grace, are you going to sit up here all night? You got a bunch of people in here for the grand opening and they want to see the brains behind 'Smoke and Stilettos". It's your baby so lets get out there so you can let all these thots know what a boss bitch looks like," my best friend Adrian said loud as hell.

She was always loud as hell. I understand her trying to talk over the music that was playing downstairs but, we were in my office. The music wasn't loud up here. I looked at my best friend and laughed. She was a chocolate goddess if I've ever seen one. She stood at five feet seven with curves to stop traffic. Her curves were real that made her all the more perfect in my eyes. She had on a Fashion Nova dress that looked like it came from one of those designers that charge four hundred dollars for a dress. It wasn't often that she stepped out of the house not put together from head to toe. She was my ace and it has always been that way.

Adrian was the opposite of me in color I was on the borderline of being brown skinned and was often called light skinned depending on the time of year. We both had our bundles and edges laid, faces beat to the gods. I was shorter than her only standing around five-foot four bare foot. My Auntie GiGi took us under her wing which is the reason we were always dressed looking like a million bucks but never spending nearly that much. The main thing that we spent astronomical amounts of money on were our shoes. We both had a killer shoe fetish. You need your feet to carry you through life so never take shorts on what you put on them is what my Auntie GiGi drilled into both of our heads. Auntie GiGi didn't have kids so we were her girls and the whole world knew it. Looking at the both of us you would never know that we had guns on us but, that was the point of having a concealed weapon permit. You had to conceal it until it was time for it to be used.

"I'm coming I'm just enjoying the view. I just wish that daddy was here to see this. He told me that this place was going to invite a bunch of hoods and criminals but, all I see is a sea of bosses just enjoying the atmosphere," I told her.

"Yeah, I miss him and his sarcastic words that he swore was solid advice," she said as she came to stand beside me.

"I did it sis. I've been working on this place for what seems like my entire life since I graduated from high school. So many people told me that it wouldn't be a reality or successful. Yet, here we are," I told her.

I remember when I first told my dad that I wanted to open a lounge that served as a cigar lounge along with a place for relaxation for the working women and men in the area. During my childhood I was always around my dad and uncles with them drinking cognac and smoking cigars. He would tell me that cigars are a man's game. It wasn't until I got older that I realized there isn't a thing that a cigar provides but, relaxation to a person. Person being the most important part. A man or a woman could smoke and have an extended knowledge of cigars. During my college years I met a lot of females that enjoyed a good ass cigar and a drink. It wasn't about being a man it was just about enjoying whatever the fuck it was that you enjoyed. For me and a lot of my friends we enjoyed cigars. As time went on the number of women smoking and being connoisseurs of cigars rose. So here we are this is the right time for me to open my place. It showed by the many people on the ground floor enjoying life and relaxing.

"I know he's proud of you. Now that's enough emotion for tonight, it's time to celebrate," she said hugging me.

She was the one person who understood the pain of losing my dad two years ago. In a lot of ways, he was her daddy too. After taking a deep breath I headed downstairs with Adrian right there beside me.

"Okay, good folks. I see the boss coming on the main floor. Everyone let's toast to the woman who started all this; the one the only Grace. Lord knows he took his time in making her. She's one of the baddest women out here mentally and physically, she proved that shit tonight by doing what it takes to make her dream a fucking reality. Cheers to you Grace and whoever made that dress and heels that you're rocking tonight. Fellas be mindful she may be single but, she damn sure ain't one of these women that you can pull with those lame ass lines you usually use. If you come at her make sure you come correct," I heard my cousin who's the DJ tonight say. I shook my head because he couldn't just introduce me, he always had to be extra with shit. Everyone clapped as I walked through. I felt a tear drop from my eyes as I received all the love. *Daddy I did it!!!*

CHAPTER 2

ully

"You ain't tell me that this was a chic's spot," I said to my right-hand Russ.

"Shit, I ain't even know. You gotta admit she did the damn thing with the place," he responded.

I nodded my head confirming. She definitely did the damn thing.

This place screamed class with how it was decorated with hardwood floors and walls. The chairs and shit were all done in matching dark blue leather fabric. The waitresses were dressed in tuxedo jackets, short skirts with some stilettos on their feet. The waiters were dressed in tuxedos as well with Stacy Adams shoes on their feet. The waitresses mainly catered to the men while the men catered to the women. They were lighting cigars and passing out drinks. The women were looking sexy as fuck and had been keeping it professional all night. I could tell that she didn't play with them just by how they were all on their game. This was definitely a place that I was going to see a lot of.

The club scene had run its course with me. The women who dressed like strippers and were steady trying to push up on you instead of doing their job was annoying as fuck. When Russ brought up that this place was opening the other day I almost didn't come. Seeing Grace float across the floor looking like a meal and a snack almost made me want to approach her ass. Yeah, I said almost because I wasn't here for that tonight plus, I wanted to see how she was moving a little bit more. She was the type of woman that commanded a room but, it wasn't because she was dressed like she was looking for a man to come at her. It was the opposite with her. She was covered up for the most part but, sexy as hell at the same time. She was a boss for damn sure. You had to give her all the props when you see her. If you didn't then you were definitely a hater. I didn't have no hater shit running in my blood. Baby girl was the shit in the best way possible. I've never been a nigga that was into a woman's feet but the way her legs looked in those heels had me wondering what she tasted like under that dress as well as what I would do to her to make her moan.

"You can put your tongue back in your mouth nigga," Russ told me laughing.

"Fuck you, how did you hear about this place?" I asked.

"Man, what the fuck you mean this is my city. The DJ is my homie, he comes to the shop on the regular. He put me on to this spot a couple of weeks ago," he told me.

"Oh yeah," I said as I continued to watch her work the crowd.

I peeped how she was drinking water in her glass instead of alcohol. I smirked because I understood the logic behind it. You can't be in control if you're tipsy. I hadn't spoken a word to this woman. She most likely isn't paying me any mind but, I'm determined to make her feel my presence before the night is over. Her wanting to be in control was obvious. That only made me want to make her lose that control even more.

"Gully! Did you hear me?" Russ said getting my attention.

"Nah, what you say?" I asked.

He gave me a funny look then gave me a head nod. I looked over to where he was gesturing to and sure enough the woman of the hour was on the floor. I had lost track of her with all the thinking I had been doing. To everyone else it looked like she was having a great time. To me though, she was out on the floor dancing around but, still peeping how things were moving around her. She wasn't any ordinary female that I already knew but, to see her still be on her boss shit and enjoy herself let me know that I had to meet her ass. I was thirsty to hear her voice, to see those lips close up, to have her say my name just so I can know what she could sound like when I take control.

"Yo, homies on break let's go get these introductions out of the way," he said tapping me on my shoulder.

As we walked to the DJ that was sitting at a table sipping on a drink there were a few people that spoke. Thirsty ass broads who licked their lips when they spoke. A few niggas trying to get some dap or some kind of acknowledgement from Russ and me. This is how it was whenever we went out. The crowd in here was more upscale but, thirst doesn't change with tax brackets. Some might say that it gets more desperate but, it was still plain old thirst to me.

"Yo Rick this is my ace Gully. Gully this is Rick the DJ and the person to tell me about this spot," Russ introduced us. We exchanged head nods. "Man, how did you end up being the DJ for the night?" He asked.

"Grace is my cousin. She didn't ask she told me that I was DJing tonight. That's lil cuz so I couldn't tell her bossy ass no. My pops would try to fight my ass if I did," he laughed.

"Damn, you got any more fine ass cousins that you're hiding? I been knowing you for a minute; I don't remember her as one of ya cousins," Russ said.

I was nodding my head to the music that was playing but, my ears were tuned in to their conversation.

"She's Uncle Greg's daughter. She's always been low-key. We tell her all the time she just needs to find a nigga to fuck that bossy shit up out of her. That's why her ass is single now. She always wants to take the lead on shit. The niggas that she's come across can't handle her, so they don't stay for long. They start out thinking that she's one of these girls that will call their cousins to handle his ass if he fucks up. Soon as they find out she don't have to call us but, they need to worry about her ass if they fuck up, they dip. I try to tell her that the boss shit that she's on is fine for outside of the house but, a man likes to be the king of the castle and shit. She's talking about ain't no kings in Virginia," he said shaking his head.

"Ain't shit wrong with that," Russ said.

"Yeah but, she doesn't know how to turn the shit off. Watch this here her ass come now," he said.

With every step she took my dick got harder. I licked my lips slow enough for her to see me. If I wasn't tipsy right now, I could swear that she licked her lips in response to me licking mine.

"Thanks for doing this for me tonight Rick," she said.

Her voice sent me off the deep end. I had to have her even if it was just for one night.

"No problem cuz, this is my homie Russ and his friend Gully," he introduced us.

"Gully? Is that the name that your mother gave you?" She asked.

"Germain is the name that she gave me," I answered.

"How bout I call you Germain then," she said.

"Whatever tickles your fancy. I'm impressed with the place you've got here. It's sexy, classy, and all that good shit. Everything is so precise and efficient," I told her.

"That's the only way to be. Being reckless and impulsive gets you nowhere,"

"Sometimes being reckless and impulsive can bring you pleasure that you've never dreamed of. You should try it sometimes," I told her as I continued to sip on my drink while eyeing her.

She gave me a smirk that showed off her dimples. I saw her eyeing my hard dick, so I shifted my stance to show her a little bit of what I was working with. She went from a smirk to a full faced smile which made me smirk.

"What is it that you do Mr. Germain?" She asked still looking at me like she wanted to eat my ass up.

"I can do it all. Are you talking about for a profession or for pleasure?" I asked.

Her cousin Rick and Russ both started coughing. I was enjoying this little game her sexy ass was playing.

"Professional of course,"

"We don't need to talk about professions. All you need to know is that I make money. It's not like we know each other personally. Unless you would like to get to know me on a personal level. If so, we can go somewhere and …. talk. I know this is your opening night so I'm not going to hold you down to any choices right now. Congratulations on the opening, you'll be seeing more of me," I told her.

"I gotta go back to work. Hit me up Russ," the DJ said before heading back to his set.

"I need a refill," Russ said before he walked off leaving Grace and I to eye fuck each other in peace.

"Is your wife or girlfriend here with you tonight?" She asked as she stepped closer to me.

"I haven't met her yet so she's not here. Well, I guess you could say she might be but, she doesn't know it yet. Where's your man?" I said stepping closer to her.

"I know you heard my cousin announce to the world that I was single," she said licking her lips.

"Oh, so you don't have a man tucked somewhere that no one knows about. I'm sure a woman as sexy as you are having a good amount of suitors coming her way,"

"Suitors? I haven't heard that word in ages," she laughed. "Men have told me that I can't be tamed so they never stay long,"

"Tamed? You're not an animal from what I can see. You may get animalistic in the right situation but, no woman can ever be tamed," I told her.

"Oh, so you don't believe that a man can break a woman so that she falls in line to let him control her?"

It took me a few minutes to think about my answer. The sexual tension between us was insane. I wanted so bad to yank her up toss her ass on the table and fuck the dog shit out of her.

"You have control and respect confused. As for a man breaking a woman, any man that breaks a woman is not a man. If he were a man, he would know that he's supposed to build a woman up the only thing a man should ever break on a woman is her back,"

She licked her lips and smiled again.

"I'm sure you can definitely break a back," she looked me up and down only making my already hard dick stand up.

"Let me know if you ever want to find out. I would buy you a drink but, water is free, and this is your spot,"

"A man that pays attention. Everyone else thinks I'm drinking white,"

I nodded my head. I appreciated the fact that she was paying attention to the fact that I was paying attention. I looked her over and she exuded confidence and she was purposeful with the words she chose. However, behind her eyes there was a lot going on that she wasn't saying. She had all my attention and that was hard for a woman to get from me. Grace was definitely someone who matched my boss.

race

I talked a little bit more to this Gully person. There was something intriguingly familiar about him. I couldn't ignore the sexiness that he possessed no matter how hard I tried. It was also evident to the other females in the lounge. They were constantly walking by saying hi and waving at his ass. It was getting on my nerves but, he was acting like it was only he and I in the entire place. That alone was attractive to me. There is nothing more attractive than a man that makes you feel like you're the only woman in the room even when you and he aren't attached to each other.

He stood taller than me even with my stilettos on. That means he has to be at least six foot three. Although I could almost guarantee he was taller than that. He had the arms of a god that were extremely noticeable under the expensive suit he had on. He didn't wear a lot of jewelry which was a plus in my book. I could see the neck tattoos slightly showing under his collar. There was also a tattoo on the back of his left hand.

The Talley and Twine watch was shining under the fluorescent lights. I smiled at the fact that when everyone was wearing Rolex's or Invicta watches he chose to support a local black owned business. That showed that he had purpose in what he spent his money on. His hands were large, and fingernails were clean. I admired his unblemished cocoa complexion and impeccable smile. The thickness of his lips made me wonder where he liked to put them and speculate on how soft they were. His eyes were chocolate, a dimple in his right cheek. Thick eyebrows, beautiful eye lashes, and his thick curly hair showed that this man was a hell of a man to look at. It wasn't often that I looked at a man and was immersed in a barrage of lust filled thoughts. None of that made any sense because this man was a stranger to me. I was going to have to ask the bartender if this was water in my glass or something else because just looking at this man made me feel high.

"Grace it's time for you to make another round in here. There are some new faces that you haven't spoken to yet," the manager of the lounge came over and told me. I turned to Gully, and he had an unreadable look on his face.

"Gully I've enjoyed our conversation but, duty calls. I want to thank you for coming out tonight now just in case I don't get back to you," I told him with a smile. He grabbed my hand sending a weird feeling straight to my pussy, he kissed the back of my hand with his soft full lips. Licking them before smiling at me to show his perfectly straight white teeth.

"By all means handle your business. I could never be a man who would stand in the way of a woman handling her shit. As far as not seeing me tonight, only time will tell how that goes. I can assure you that you will be seeing me again in the near future. Congratulations again on your grand opening," he told me.

I turned to walk away from him. Once he was out of my sight, I released the air that I was holding in my lungs.

"I think he has an itch that he wants you to scratch," Dasia said with a smile.

"Do you know him or anything about him? He came with a guy named Russ," I asked her.

I knew that Russ was friends with my cousin but, I had never heard him mention the name Gully. It was crazy how I knew most of my cousins' friends just by him talking about them most of the time. I never was the girl cousin that hung with the boy cousins just to get with their friends. I kept myself separate from their friends or whatever activities they had going on. I only met people if they would bring them around the family. As I was saying I had heard of Russ because he was the one that ran a shop of some sort. I never really paid attention but, now I wished I had.

"I don't know him but, I can check around and find out what I can. He damn sure looks like a boss with and annihilate the pussy type of dick. His pants weren't even tight, and that monster was peeking at your ass," she said laughing.

I didn't respond to her due to the fact that I didn't know her on that level. She seemed to be a cool person but, nah her and I didn't chop it up like that so there was no need to start doing it now.

"Your father would be proud of you Grace. This place turned out to be way more than he thought it would be. You did really good baby," my uncle told me followed by him giving me a kiss on the cheek.

"Thank you Unc. I've been thinking about him off and on all week. It hurts that he isn't here to see it though,"

"Oh, his big head ass is here. You think he would let something like death keep him away from here. I feel his presence here just like you do. Now that you have one of your goals out of the way. When are you gonna give me some grand-nieces and nephews for me to spoil? I'll even let them call me Uncle-Granddaddy," he said laughing.

My Uncle Geoff was just as handsome as my dad and his other two brothers. They were all tall. I think Uncle Geon was the shortest but, he was six feet even so that's not considered short to the average person. Although their ages ranged from forty-nine to fifty-four, they didn't look half of that. No gray hair in sight, all of them had hazel brown eyes, and fat cheeks with dimples. Uncle Geoff was the one that looked the most like my father. I guess the fact that they were project twins; they were eleven months apart in age; was a major factor in that. He was also the uncle that I was the closest too. He stayed with me for a month and a half after my father died. Having him here tonight meant so much to me. Family is what kept me going most of the time. With a family like mine there was no way I wasn't going to succeed at any task in life.

"That's not on my list. I think you have your list and mine combined. Children are not in the cards for me,"

"Yes, they are you just gotta open ya eyes and pay attention. The man that will make you forget all that hot shit you talk to these knuckleheads that don't know how to handle a woman like you."

"Handle me? I'm just fine handling myself thank you," I said tilting my head to the side with a smile.

"Trust me my dear sweet niece there is a man out there that will gladly break your boss ass down. I just hope I'm still alive to see the shit go down," he said with his signature chuckle.

"Auntie GiGi says otherwise,"

"You keep listening to her. She missed her boat but, you betta not miss yours," he said before walking away.

I stood there trying to think of when I had seen a man with Auntie GiGi at all. Whenever I was around it was always just us girls unless the uncles came around. Come to think of it she never said anything about a date or nothing. I couldn't think about that right now. I had to finish my night out with a bang. The people were coming in still even though it was after one in the morning. We closed at four, so I was on the countdown now. From the looks of all the smiles these people were gonna be here until closing time.

"I'm proud of you," I heard.

The voice made me roll my eyes. I don't understand how a man can call himself a boss or a player and carry himself as the exact opposite of both. I turned to see my ex-boyfriend and pain in my ass. Blaine Johnson was on the outside an average height light skinned, curly haired, brown eyed, smooth talking black guy. On the inside however, he's as white as his name was. He was the epitome of a walking identity crisis. He was raised in one of the richest neighborhoods in his hometown. He attended the finest schools, wore the finest clothes, drove the finest cars, and only ate at the finest restaurants. All of which he constantly reminded me of. He was a stockbroker that did extremely well for himself, also something he reminded me of. I had forgotten that he knew about my grand opening. I gave him a forced smile.

"Blaine how nice of you to come. I wasn't expecting to see you here, it's a surprise," I told him as I handed him my hand for him to kiss the back of it.

"I had to come and show my support for you. I still have my doubts about the neighborhood you chose to put this place in. Nonetheless, I think that it will do these inner-city kids some good to see a black owned business whose success doesn't revolve around them accepting food stamps as payment," he said.

That right there is the reason why we couldn't stay together. He was really a sweetheart if you take away all the condescending shit that came out of his mouth.

"Have you been here long?" I asked attempting to change the subject.

"Not long, I may stay for a few more minutes but, I would hate for something to happen to my Aston Martin in the parking lot," he said adjusting his suit jacket.

"It was so nice seeing you but, I have things to handle by all means get back to your precious car," I told him walking away quickly so he couldn't say anything else to me. I needed to do something to stop myself from taking a drink of anything more than water tonight. I didn't need to have any alcohol in my system because I needed to be on my shit tonight. Now when we close that would be another story. I planned on having a few drinks at the bar just to celebrate and reflect on the road that led me here.

OOOOO

It was quiet as hell and almost six in the morning when I found myself sitting at the bar with a glass of *1738* and the bottle sitting beside it. The sounds of Trina were playing, and I was relaxed for a change. At this moment there wasn't a fire for me to put out, a fake smile to push, or even an imitation laugh to a bad joke. Right now, I was just Grace something I hadn't been in a long time. It seemed like my father getting sick and dying while I was putting this place together made me lose myself. I had always heard of women losing themselves because of a man, a family, a job, and even something as superficial as trying to please others. I had lost myself because of grief and my choice to run from it instead of stopping to handle it like I should have. Now my father was buried, and my dream had become a reality now there was nothing for me to get distracted with or even to try to avoid. It had been two years and here I was grieving the death of my superhero on a night I should still be smiling.

ully

"Is that everything?" I asked Russ.

"Yeah," he answered.

"Good looking out y'all for hanging back and helping me load up my equipment. I didn't think I would just be going home from this gig this time of morning when she said it was a cigar lounge. I admit the shit was lit as fuck in there. I'm happy everything turned out great for her," he said.

"Yeah, where is she though? Her car is the only one in the parking lot besides ours. I can't believe she doesn't have security here to walk her out at night. I know it's not the worst part of the hood but, it's still hood," I said.

I admit I only stayed behind so I could get to talk to her some more. Russ was my dude and all but, me helping these niggas load up equipment with my expensive gear on wasn't normal for me. Russ and the DJ guy whose name I still didn't know looked at each other.

"Man, look I don't know you like this nigga does but, if he says you're solid then you must be. I see you got a thing for my cousin. She's not like other chic's, never has been. She was basically raised by her pops, my aunt and my uncles. If you plan on running game or making her a part of the stable don't even, try. She'll eat you alive and have you rethinking life strategies and shit. I'm not gonna tell you not to hurt her because no nigga has gotten that close to her to even try to hurt her," he told me.

"Damn, she can't be that bad."

"I'll put it to you like this. Her tt best friend have nicknames that we gave them but, will never call them that shit to their faces. We call them Fire and Ice. Grace is Ice."

"Damn."

"But hey, she's still inside sitting at the bar. I only know because I have the cameras for the club linked to my phone. It's only me, her, and my pops that can see the cameras though," he said giving me a head nod. We dapped each other up and he got in his truck, Russ got in his whip and I took my black ass in the lounge to see how thick the ice was. He was right because she was sitting at the bar just like he said. I stopped when I heard Trina holler about being the baddest bitch. Seeing her listening to Trina was amusing as fuck to me. They didn't seem to mix but, maybe she had an inner bitch that loved to suck and fuck underneath all that boss exterior. Just the thought of her throwing it back and crying out in pleasure for me to stop made my dick hard.

"You need to get some security to walk you out if you plan on staying here alone after y'all close," I told her.

When she turned to face me with a face wet with tears and eyes full of pain a nigga felt funny. I always hated seeing women cry but, this wasn't that normal feel bad feeling. I felt like I needed to be the one to fix those tears and repair whatever pain had caused them. She looked at me but, stayed quiet.

Her tears were looking like waterfalls dropping down her face. She didn't look like the, in control boss that I had met a few hours ago. This woman sitting before me was not only broken but, she was lost. I took a seat beside her. She turned back to her glass that she was nursing. Seeing her this way didn't stop me from wanting to know more about her. Shit, I could still see myself being with her when the time was right.

"I thought everyone had left. Why are you still here?" She asked lowly.

"I was helping your cousin load up his stuff. They left and I know I couldn't leave you here alone. I didn't expect to see you in here nursing a bottle. What's good? It's better if you talk about it rather than leave it in."

"I don't even know you."

"Sometimes the fact that we just met can help you out. Think about it this way. You can tell me some shit about somebody, and you're all confused trying to decide what the next move should be. The one thing that's holding you back is the fact that you're attached to whomever. With attachment comes feelings. It doesn't matter if there's no romantic or physical attachment, it still brings feelings. Feelings bring doubt and second guessing your first mind. With me being a stranger, I don't have none of that. Whoever it is that you talk about is nothing but a faceless name. I don't owe them any loyalty at all. That means I can see shit that your feelings and attachments hide."

"I just want to be happy and have my dad back. Too bad my dad died and there ain't a man out here that can handle me. Every relationship ends because they say that I'm too much like a man. I think like a man, make business moves like a man, I even think about sex like a man. Sex is just an action between two people who need a release nothing more nothing less. Men get intimidated by me and want to make me scale back how I move just to help their ego stay in tack. I can't do that, and I shouldn't have to."

"You're right you should never alter a damn thing about you for anyone but, you. As for all that bullshit you just said about men and all that; the right one will love to see you on your boss shit. Only a weak nigga will ask you to tame anything about you. A real one will be only trying to control his hard dick when you're on your boss shit. You can't say that you've been striking out with men when you've only been dealing with male humans with the minds of teenage boys. When you get in a relationship you should be with someone who not only matches your boss status but, will push you and place you in positions that will enhance that shit to its full potential.

"Let me break it down for you if you were my woman and you came to me saying you wanted to do some shit like buy a mall or some shit. We'll sit down, talk it out just so I can see if you really want the shit or if you're just talking. Once it's established that you're serious then I get in action calling around trying to see what's for sale and all that good shit. You can still be doing what you need to do as well. You know like getting the business plan together, finding out the process of getting stores to agree to rent the space in the mall you know the leg work. Once the leg work is done then we go looking at the places. You pick and I pay. A relationship is a partnership where we both are equal. Where I'm weak you pick up the slack and vice versa. No one person is dominate because if that happens it's no longer a relationship but, a dictatorship. If a man can't help and encourage what the hell is he there for?"

"That all sounds good but, things never turn out the way you want them to. It's all a part of life. I can't expect for people to always have my best interest in mind. Even if I'm in a relationship I can't assume that the person wants the best for me," she said.

"If you're in a relationship with anyone then that shouldn't ever be an issue. I'm not just talking about a romantic relationship either. I know for me I'm not gonna enter into a business, personal, or leisure friendship with you if I don't trust that you won't do anything to harm me." I told her.

She was listening to what I said but, it wasn't changing her feelings about anything that much I could tell. She was a hard female to get to. Most females would eat up anything I had to say. I could tell some of them that I was a Russian with a tan and they would believe me. I should've known that Grace isn't like any of them. She was straight forward and in no way gullible. I watched her kill the rest of the drink that was in front of her.

"That all sounds good. Unfortunately, I don't have all the answers. If I did, I wouldn't be here alone nursing alcohol," she said.

I watched her as she stood up shakily and tried to avoid looking at me. I blocked her path, placed my hand underneath her chin to lift her face to force her to look at me. She was gonna stop with the bullshit. I don't know what she was expecting but, I can bet a million dollars that she wasn't ready for what she was about to get.

"Have you ever not been in control?" I asked as I stepped closer to her.

The strong smell of the liquor she was drinking didn't stop my mind from wondering what her moans and sex faces were like. The tears building in her eyes didn't stop me from wanting to dig so deep inside of her that I didn't need to ask her shit. I was gonna know what made her lose control. I was gonna be the one to make her give me control.

"Not having control is not an option. The control protects me from getting hurt," she said to me.

I knew there was a reason she was holding on to control so damn tight. She was scared of being hurt when she needed to realize that she was already broken.

CHAPTER 5

race

This is not how my night is supposed to end. I was too intoxicated to have this man behind me right now. I was trying to get another bottle from the bar and here he was standing right behind me. I could feel his breath on my neck. My eyes were closed, and I was enjoying the feeling of his hands roaming my body freely.

"You're so fucking soft," he whispered. His hands unzipped my dress. This was insane I was behind the bar with my Balmain two-thousand-dollar dress in a pile surrounding my feet. I was expecting him to say something smart about the fact that I didn't have on panties or a bra. Yes, right now this man had me in just heels. "Hell, motherfucking yeah, the lord did the damn thing when he made you Grace. I see why your name is Grace. Woman I want all the grace and mercy that you have to give tonight."

The liquor caused me to be a little looser with my mouth than I would normally be.

"Are you gonna fuck me 'til I cum or talk to me 'til I cum?" I asked.

Out of nowhere he smacked me on the ass but, before I could protest his hand was around my neck and his mouth was directly on my ear.

"Bend over and spread those sexy ass legs. I need to show you who the fuck is in charge. It doesn't matter to me the rougher the better. If you wanna battle me I'm sure I'll come out the winner. BEND THE FUCK OVER," he commanded.

My body folded right there in front of this man. I heard him taking his pants off. The excitement that filled my body as I anticipated him entering me was astronomical. Not even opening my dream lounge matched it. This man did things to my body I have never experienced or could hope for. He took his finger and traced it along my spine at a snail's pace. Out of nowhere he lifted me up and put me on top of the bar. So here I was bent over on top of the bar with my ass facing him and legs hanging down. I felt some liquid drip over my ass cheeks. The surprise was the fact that he was face deep between those cheeks. He was pouring the liquor and slurping the liquor, my ass, and my pussy at the same time. I was squirming and moving around because he was busting through my walls that I had built up around me.

"Shit," I called out. He smacked my ass squeezing both cheeks at the same time.

"If you not calling my name keep that shit to yourself," he barked at me.

The sound of his voice brought the climax on that he had been working for. I screamed incoherently as he gobbled up every-thing I had to give at the moment. I was wrong in thinking that the release would help him go about his way. He rolled me over so that my back was now on the bar with him standing between my legs with his shirt on. I wondered what his bare chest looked like until he started playing with my nipples. Yet again he poured liquor on my naked skin. He caught all he could with his mouth. Just when I began to enjoy the feeling of his mouth on my skin, he entered me.

"Oh shit!" I yelled out.

"Why the fuck you so damn tight? You're trying to kill a nigga," he said as he looked down on me. He slow stroked me until my walls loosened up a little bit. Once I was more comfortable with his size and length, he started talking cold cash shit. "Boss chics have the best fucking pussy. This shit is fucking priceless," he said as he pummeled my core over and over again. I was trying to look everywhere but into his eyes. It felt like he knew all the secrets that I didn't tell anyone when he looked at me. The combination of him being inside me and looking deep into my soul had me ready to surrender to him and only him. If I didn't look at him, he wouldn't be able to see all that just by our eyes connecting. *Maybe he wasn't feeling what I was feeling.*

"Gully don't stop. Right there baby," I moaned.

He didn't say a damn thing he just kept staring at me. He knew what the hell he was doing. There ain't no way I can be feeling all these emotions and his cocky ass doesn't feel shit. Nah this whatever it was between us was thick in the air. At first, I thought it was sexual tension but, here he is balls deep inside me and I still feel something in the air.

"Look at me Grace," he told me as he gripped my hips.

When I looked at him there it was again. That fucking feeling again, now it was in addition to the increased speed of my heart beating. Why was I compelled to tell this man that I love him? I don't know him. I have to stop drinking all together. *Is it the drinks or the man? It just might be the man. When I drink alone I usually just go to sleep. I don't even pull out the toy in the top of my closet. It has to be him because even when I was drinking water I wanted to fuck. Yeah, that's what it is he's my kryptonite, in other words he's my Mr. Wrong. Is he wrong though?*

"Mmmmm," I moaned out.

"Stop thinking all the fucking time. Catch this nut I'm about to throw to your sexy ass," he told me pulling me from my thoughts. "Shit, fuck," he said as he slammed into me. I could feel him releasing his seeds into my tunnel. He just came inside me, a stranger that I just met tonight, just came inside me. Any other day or time I would be on my feet cursing his ass out. Yet again this man had me not wanting him to pull out of me at all. There's no way I could be okay with this thot ass scenario that I was in right now.

Once he finished his release, he stood me up smooth as hell. I found myself getting tongued down and groped. I was loving every bit of it. I was actually ready for a night of nonstop love making. He had just slid out of me and here it is I was about to beg this nigga for some more dick. Instead of begging him verbally, I slid down to my knees and decided to try my hand to make his ass beg instead. He was quiet as I picked his dick up with my tongue instead of my hands. I looked up at him as I licked my remnants off of him. *Yeah Mr. Gully you're in for a treat that no one has received from me.*

I started bobbing my head up and down applying the right amount of pressure at the right time. His hand went to my head immediately. Since my hands were free, they went to work on his balls. I started making loud slurping and sucking noises as I sped up my pace. I looked up at him to see that he was barely hanging on. I removed his dick from my mouth still looking at him. It was like we were both under some sort of dick sucking spell. I was trying to break him while at the same time he was trying to prove that a blowjob can't break him. I let some spit drop from my mouth onto his dick not breaking eye contact. He bit his lip, licked his lips, then bit his lip again. *There's the first crack.* I did it a few more times all while playing with his balls and jerking him with my hands. Without warning I took him into my mouth again. This time I was sucking him with speed, pressure, and enjoying the fact that I had no gag reflex. Finally, his head went back breaking the starring contest that we had going on.

"Hell yeah," he called out as he looked at the ceiling. I welcomed his release into my mouth as if it was my aunties macaroni and cheese. "Damn woman, shit," he said as I sucked even harder trying to get every damn drop of his goodness. Once the climax was over, he stood me up so I could face him. The look he was giving me had my pussy thumping waiting on some more Gully Dick.

"Was that okay?" I asked just to see what his response was going to be. He licked those sexy ass lips again.

"You got an office in this motherfucker?" He asked. I nodded my head up and down and he picked up my dress from the floor, stepped to the side. "Lead the way."

He slapped me on the ass as I did just that. I guess my grand opening wasn't going to be the best thing that happened to me this weekend.

ully

A month and a half later

"In order for the shipment to come on time we have to have the proper people riding with the shipment. I recommend someone that you can trust not to run off with your shit," Calero said.

Any other time I would knock his fucking head off for coming at me like I'm some damn amateur. He was trying the fuck out of me today. He knew I wasn't on top of my shit today. I hadn't been on top of shit since I left that fucking lounge in the wee hours of the morning the next day. I had fucked all the drunkenness out of Grace, so I wasn't worried about her getting home safe or no shit like that. I had came inside her quicksand pussy over five damn times and didn't regret any of it. I didn't know what to make of the night we had. My emotions were all over the fucking place that night. I'm habitually a fuck and duck kind of guy. I couldn't get enough of Grace; I still wanted some more of her right now. She's the reason Calero wasn't bleeding and crying right now.

"I suggest you find another mother fucker to try today Calero. We all know that I'm a lot of things but, a rookie and green to how shit gets done aren't on the list. The next time you try to throw some shade from a tree at me I'll bury your ass under that motherfucker. Are we clear?" I asked. He nodded his head up and down. "Nah, don't get mute on me now. Use your fucking words. That way I won't have to guess if that nod was in English, Spanish or whatever the fucking language is where you come from."

"It's understood Gully."

"Get the fuck out of my office."

He got up and walked out too scared to look back at me. I went over to my bar and poured me a glass of *1738*. Hennessy and D'usse were mostly what I preferred to drink. However, since that night I drank *1738* off of Grace's skin that's all I've had a taste for. I hadn't reached out to her since that night and it's been over a month. I needed some time to get my head together after how I felt that night. Something had to be wrong with me. There's no way I caught feelings for a broad I didn't know. I'm saying all I knew was what her cousin told us, her name, and that she owned the lounge we were at. There's no way I could be ready to give her the world including my last name. I haven't touched or thought about another chic at all since then. I'm barely sleeping due to the fact that I end up fucking her every night in my dreams. I haven't beat my dick so much since I was in junior high school. Here it is I was beating my shit at least twice a day thinking about her ass. I had to see her tonight though. I couldn't take this shit anymore. I had to lay my eyes on her, not fuck her, just see her.

Being the man that I am I just can't allow her to think she has me by the balls even if she does. I was gonna go by her club tonight but, I wasn't going alone. The fact that she hasn't even tried to get in contact with me bothered me a bit. I know I gave her some good maybe even great dick that night. I suppose it wasn't good enough for her to even send me a smoke signal. If she was unfazed by the connection, I felt that we had then, it was going to stay that way. I'm not a nigga that runs behind any woman. I had too many of them trying to get me to shoot them up with some babies for me to only be worried about Grace. I was in unfamiliar territory with how I was feeling and thinking about her. I never thought I would be at this point. I was thinking about her at random times during the day, dreaming about her, and even brought cases of a liquor that I didn't drink just because of that one night.

"Yo, Gully! What the fuck is up with you man? Who the fuck we gotta go kill?" Russ asked.

"When the fuck did you get here? The days of killing mother fuckers are over for me. What you doing here?" I asked him.

"Nigga, I've been here for about ten minutes calling your damn name. Where the fuck was your head?" He asked.

Russ and I went back but, I wasn't about to tell him that Grace had my head fucked up.

"Thinking about this acquisition deal that I have on the table. It's for three hundred acres of land deep in Suffolk. It's damn near in North Carolina it's so damn close to the state line. The developer wants to put some apartments or condos on it. The land alone is gonna cost them six hundred thousand bucks. If they stay with our company and let the architecture firm build them motherfuckers, we stand to make a shit load of money. Then I had Calero try me this morning with his Italian sub smelling ass. I know I'm gonna have to hang the suit up to deal with him sooner than later. He thinks because I took a back seat to shit that he can come at me and not have to deal with the consequences," I told Russ.

"Man, leave his fat ass alone. The last thing you need right now is a problem with the folks that his sloppy ass is tied to. We've been out of the streets for seven years now. Straight up we don't even need to continue dabbling in the shit that we are in. Look around nigga we got out of all that street shit. What nigga you know that we came up with that's the CEO and CFO of a multimillion-dollar conglomerate. We own the top three floors of this fucking building and you're pissed that a fat sloppy nigga came at you wrong. Fuck him and his sub making mama. Gully we're good man let that shit go. What did he come at you about anyway?"

"He tried to tell me that I needed someone I trust on the shipment. I should've slapped the taste out of his mouth,"

"Petty shit. I say you call up his uncle and tell him to keep his shipment and all the rest of them motherfuckers too. He ain't worth the unwanted heat that fucking him up would bring. We can pay them for two shipments so they can leave us the fuck alone,"

Russ was right for a change. It was usually me talking to him about us pulling out completely. We've been just strictly suppling for damn near six years. It was long overdue for us to put that shit to rest. We were reaping the benefits of our real estate and land brokerage firm in addition to the businesses that we were backing all around the city. We made money sleeping, and on the fucking toilet. There wasn't a need for us to continue to take the risk of being the suppliers anymore.

"Set up a meeting with fat ass and his uncle. Even though his nephew is fat, sloppy, and stinking we need to tell Unc what our future plans are."

"Didn't fat ass just leave here? Why you can't call him? I hate talking to him on the phone. He's always breathing all hard and shit like he just got finished running when we all know his ass is sitting down," Russ laughed.

Calero was indeed a fat ass he was barely five feet six inches but, he weighed over three hundred pounds. He would sweat and smell just like a sub sandwich. I didn't see how he pulled women. No, that's a lie I know he pulled the chics that he did because he was connected to people who had money and power. I understood why Russ didn't like talking to him because I didn't like dealing with him either. We were in this to make money not friends, so shit had to get handled.

"Don't play with me."

"I'll call his fat ass. I hope he doesn't get hungry and eat the phone before I call though," Russ joked.

"What else is going on with ya?"

"Not shit. I had to come lay eyes on you and make sure you were good. You've been quiet the last couple of weeks. You never said what happened when you went back in the lounge to take Grace's fine ass home,"

"Ain't shit to tell. She was drunk as fuck though. I made sure she was straight then I dipped," I told him.

He looked at me like he knew that I was leaving some shit out. There wasn't a need to tell him about the one night I had with Grace. The lack of communication afterwards showed that it was just a one-night stand nothing more, nothing less.

OOOOOO

"I thought we were going to a club, like a real club," Nita said as we walked into *Smoke and Stilettos*.

"Don't remind me of why I don't bring you out in public tonight. Just sit back and enjoy the night. This maybe something new and different for you but, make sure you leave the thot behavior in the parking lot," I told her as we took our seats.

She mumbled under her breath because she knew not to try me with some hot shit coming out of her mouth. Sha'Nita was a female that was aware she was on the fuck roster. She didn't mind so there were never any issues about what we had going on. Tonight, when I called, I was fully expecting her to tell me to go fuck myself. She happily agreed to come with me to the lounge as nothing more than eye candy. I left out the part that she was just a prop to get a reaction out of Grace. I couldn't show up tonight solo. Grace had to see that life went on with or without her. Was this considered game playing? I'm sure you could say that I was playing games but, I call it research. I need to see where her head is regarding me.

"Can I be a thot when we leave here?" Nita asked smartly.

"Later for all that bullshit. I don't understand how y'all females always want to go out with a nigga but, when you do you got complaints and questions. Life is less complex when my dick is in your mouth," I told her.

Nita was the closest competition for Grace in the looks and body departments. As for everything else Grace killed her ass. Nita's aspirations didn't reach any further then driving some hood nigga's car to impress her bird ass friends. Her pussy was on its way to holding a drive-thru movie event. She served her purpose for a nut and nothing more.

"Good Evening, Mr. Gully. My name is Monica and I will be your waitress tonight. Welcome to Smoke and Stilettos. The owner sent over a bottle of *1738* with two glasses for you and your lady friend. The owner would like for me to let you know that everything is free to you," Monica told me.

I looked at the bottle and I could feel me getting pissed that Grace would try to play me like this. She maybe a sexy woman with the best box that my dick has been in but, she had some balls on her as well.

"Let the owner know that I will accept her offer and whatever else she has to offer," I told her.

I could feel Nita's eyes burning a hole in the side of my face.

race

I smirked when Monica told me about Gully's little message. It was obvious that he thought bringing whatever she was to him in my establishment tonight was going to get me to address him and his need for attention. It most certainly was not. Seeing him brought the flashbacks that I had been experiencing since that night. I stood at the window in my office watching him interact with her, eat the food that I was so graciously providing to them. He would look around no doubt looking for me. Since he wanted to fuck with me it was my turn to fuck with him.

"Here are the cigars that you requested ma'am," Sandino said as he sat the box on my desk.

"Thank you," I smiled.

I know I said he wasn't going to see me but, the petty levels in me wanted or needed to show my face to him and his little toy for the night. I signed the card, took a deep breath and headed to the table that they occupied. When I approached, I could see her face coated with envy. Imagine that I hadn't even said a word yet and she already felt some type of way.

"Gully, it's so nice to see you give my humble establishment another try."

"I told you that I would come back. I'm a man of many things but, most importantly I'm a man of my word. You look nice tonight," he said as he raped me with his eyes. He was sure to lick his lips a few times making my pussy start thumping.

"I just wanted to personally deliver a cigar to you that I felt would suit your tastes. It's a part of the *Caldwell Lost & Found* limited collection. It's one of the newer lines that I've chosen to carry. I have tried one and it's definitely exquisite and memorable. It's called *One Night Stand*. I'm sure a man of your caliber has taken part of his fair share of one-night stands," I told him.

His escort coughed in an effort to remind him that she was sitting there. We had been engaged in a silent conversation.

"Are you not going to introduce me, Gully?"

"Why would I introduce you to anybody I fuck with on the regular? You're not my girl we just hang out from time to time. It ain't even enough for you to be over there fake choking. Back to you Grace. I'll be sure to let you know how this one-night stand goes."

"Don't do me any favors. I'm just here to provide you with the best tasting cigars that have ever been between your lips. If you don't like it, I will take that into consideration when I make my next order. I hope you both enjoy your night," I said with a smile then headed back to my office.

I can imagine what the rest of the night's discussion was going to be. I was engrossed in paperwork when my door was opened.

"Where the hell did you find a cigar named one-night stand?" He asked.

He had an amused expression on his face. I took some time to appreciate the view a man that knew how to make a suit come alive. The way the dark blue Tom Ford suit with the black silk shirt underneath the jacket was holding on to him for dear life is a vision that dreams are made of. He was standing in front of the desk with his hands in his pockets. I could've avoided looking at his dick but, what the hell. I looked at it licking my lips causing him to chuckle.

"I'm in the cigar business Germain. I can tell you that there is a cigar out there that will fit every occasion or event that you can think of. Is there a problem with your drinks or food?" I asked.

"No, why would there be?"

"I'm just inquiring because there has to be a reason why you left your guest to come to my office."

He didn't talk to me but, he took my phone of the desk. I sat and watched as he typed then put it back.

"You don't have a lock on your phone?"

"If you just picked it up to do whatever you did then you know I don't have a lock on it."

"That wasn't a question it was a statement. You have to keep somethings tucked away from the rest of the world. Using a lock on your phone can accomplish that."

"I don't have a need to lock anything. I don't have a man that I answer to. I don't do a lot of things on my phone that other people do so there's no need to lock anything. I'm an open book."

"What about your legs and your heart? Are they an open book as well?"

"The only legs and heart you need to concern yourself with are at the table waiting on you. You really should be getting back to her," I told him.

"For what? She's not going anywhere."

"Cockiness is not sexy all the time."

"I know but, that wasn't cockiness. It was and will always be the truth. I could fuck you on the table in front of her and she'll be there when I call for her to top me off," he said nonchalantly.

"Is that the type of woman you want?"

"No, she's just available," he answered with a shrug.

"Interesting."

"Not as interesting as me pouring her a glass of *1738* wishing I was pouring it all over you instead. It's nice to see that you're still going ahead with business as usual."

"Why wouldn't I? Although your sex is memorable, it's not earth shattering or even on the levels of stopping the progress of my day," I lied.

"Stand up and come here for a minute," He said not addressing what I just said.

"For what?"

"I know you're not scared to come closer to me. I'm just saying since my sex game ain't shit," he said with a smile. I got up and moved to the side of the desk that he was on. I tried to play it smart by not getting to close to him. He read right through my attempt by immediately stepping into my space. To have him in such a close proximity to my body caused my mouth to dry. I took a deep breath trying to control my body's response to him. He moved his face close to mine, my eyes closing involuntarily. I was anticipating a kiss instead I felt the heat of his breath on my ear. "I never took you to be a liar, Grace. Your mouth said all that bullshit but, right now your body is screaming for my touch. No matter how much you try to keep your body from speaking; I hear it loud and clear. Don't worry my dick and mouth are calling out for your pussy too with her moist ass. Don't get it twisted I'm not a man that has to beg and plead for shit. However, for you I'll go down there get on the mic and tell the world that I'm having dreams of being knee deep inside of you. But, you in here playing," he said then he walked out of the office.

He knows damn well my pussy was sopping wet craving his touch and love but, he walked his ass out of here. I guess it was good that he left when he did because I would have gone against every rule that I had set up in my life and rode his dick until we both got the relief that we were both craving. It wasn't going to matter that he had that female here with him tonight. I would send him back to her empty and no longer horny. I had to keep my distance from Germain. He was bound to be trouble for me. I wasn't a weak woman and I didn't need a man however, when it came to Germain I was as weak as they come. That wasn't a good thing, not for me.

OOOO

The ringing of the phone took me from a deep sleep that was dearly needed. I reached over with my eyes still closed grabbing the phone I opened one eye to press the green button.

"Hello," I groaned.

"Grace you gotta get to General Hospital. Daddy just had a heart attack," Rick said into the phone. I sat straight up in the bed. My heart began to beat fast; palms became sweaty in an instant. I could feel the tears starting to pool in my eyes. Uncle Geoff was always the one I could talk to there's no way the lord could be taking him away from me so soon. After losing my father, I never wanted to step into that hospital again. Unfortunately, it was the best hospital in the area. "Grace, what the fuck is you doing man? Did you hear what I just said?"

"I fucking heard you Rick. I'm on my way," I told him ending the call.

I took a few deep breaths and whipped the tears away that had already fallen. *Get your ass in gear Grace. You have to be there with the family. Uncle Geoff needs you to be there. Not going is not an option.*

I was able to put my clothes on and get to the car without breaking down. The ride there I had the radio on because the last thing I needed right now was quiet. I needed the distraction which doesn't make much sense because I wasn't really paying it any attention. I got to the parking lot of the hospital way quicker than I was supposed to. I parked the car and just sat there looking at the building. This was the building that I last spoke to my father in. The last time I kissed him on the cheek, held his hand, and heard his voice. I never wanted to come here again there were nothing but bad memories here for me.

Lord please wrap your arms around Uncle Geoff. I know it's been two years since you took my father. It still seems too close for you to take his brother now. I pray that this is just a setback for our family. I know with you we can get through all things but, please don't take him away from me too. Please don't, not now, I don't know how I'll be able to handle it if you do, amen. After saying the prayer, I got out of the car. This is going to take a lot out of me but, I'm not going anywhere until I find out what is going on with Uncle Geoff.

When I reached the waiting area, I quickly saw that my family are the only ones in the waiting room. I know there are more family members than what was in here but, we still were the only ones in the room. Looking around I could see the worry and anguish on everyone's face.

"Grace, he's still in surgery. He's been in there for an hour already. I don't know how much longer it will be," My Auntie GiGi said.

"I know Auntie GiGi. I'll be here just like the rest of y'all until we find out what's going on," I told her.

I took a seat and prayed that everything would be okay.

ully

"Thank you for allowing our company to complete your project. As I said before for the duration of the project you can always just swing by to see how things are progressing. If you come and have some concerns about the progress or anything else concerning the project you can always reach out to the foreman on sight or call me. You will never feel like you're out of the loop."

"I appreciate the openness that your company exhibits during your projects. After being in the business for so long there are some companies that will only allow you on the work site if you have an appointment. That leaves room for the customer to start to have doubts on the efficiency of the workers," Mr. Fletcher told me.

"That's exactly why we don't function that way. There's no room for a company to build and gain more clients if the clients they already have don't trust them. Any relationship business or otherwise is built on trust," I replied.

Mr. Fletcher nodded his head in agreement. I was only speaking what I knew to be true. I didn't care if he did or did not agree. We had a way of doing things around here and they weren't changing any time soon. I knew when he first met me, he felt like I was just another street nigga looking for a come up by starting this company. He was partially right but, with me starting my company was always the end game to the street shit that I used to do. I was used to people judging and having misconceptions about me and my company as a whole. It wasn't until they actually started doing business with me that they realized this isn't a passing phase or a hobby with me. It's about leaving a legacy and a way for my children to have something to work for instead of them just growing up to work for someone else.

"I appreciate you acknowledging that fact. Well, I will get on out of here and let you get to work. I have a feeling this isn't the last time we will do business with each other," he told me as he held out his hand for me to shake.

"I don't have a problem with that."

I watched as he walked out of the office. This was going to be a great thing for the company. This project along with the land deal that was about to be closed was going to indeed put us on the map. I sat back in my chair thinking of how just five years ago this was nothing more than a dream. The fellas on the street would give me bullshit about how I moved when I was out there. The only thing I did that was the same as other drug dealers was have a steady roster of willing pussy. I didn't stay in the high-class part of town, the most expensive car that I drove was a regular ass Benz. Although I stayed fresh as far as my clothes went, I didn't go all out and pay hundreds of dollars for some regular ass jeans and shirts. I was never the real flashy type but, I made sure my shit wasn't raggedy as fuck either. All that sacrificing I did was now paying off. I wasn't Gully the nigga that every street nigga wanted to be. I was Germain the nigga with a few companies that he started which are all successful. Now the only thing I needed was someone to share all this success with. Grace could be the one but, she's still on the fence about how she was going to proceed with me. I was a patient nigga and had nothing but, time on my hands. My office door opened and in walked the last person I wanted to see, especially while I was in a great mood. Just looking at her I knew that shit was bound to change.

"Aren't you looking as handsome as ever," she said with a smile.

"Martina what are you doing here?" I asked ignoring her bull-shit ass compliment.

Martina was once the head pussy on the pussy roster. That was saying something at the time. She was always there for me to relieve some stress regardless of her being married at the time. Her husband was always out of town for this and that so to her he was never an issue. Everything was fine between us until she started getting too attached. I had to explain to her that I was never her or anyone else's side nigga. She was only another pussy for me to fuck at the end of the day. Even with her being the head pussy she was just as replaceable as the others. She started acting out of pocket, so I replaced her. It's been a little over a year since I had seen or heard from her, so I was confused as to why she was here at all.

"Why don't you look like you're happy to see me?"

"I'm still waiting for you to answer the question."

"My brother is looking to buy some land," she said.

"What does that have to do with me?"

"You're one of the newest up and coming land brokers in the city. I would like for you to work with him. He needs all the help he can get. Although he's extremely smart he knows nothing about acquiring land," she said.

"We're unable to take on another project at this time. I'm sure there are other land brokers that would gladly help him out."

What I just told her wasn't a complete lie. Yes, we had two major projects that we were working on now but, I could work with her brother if I wanted to. The problem is that I don't want to work with anyone attached to Martina. I didn't need me working with her people giving her any ideas of me fucking her again. I was good on her and her pussy.

"I'm sure you could squeeze him in. If memory serves me correctly you could do whatever it is that you wanted to do. If you wanted to do this favor for an old friend, I'm sure you would find a way," she said as she crossed her legs.

"Like I said we can't help him right now," I said sternly.

"Well, I guess I can say that I tried. It's a shame though," she said as she stood up.

"Yeah, I bet," I replied.

"It was good seeing you though Germain," she stated.

"Gully, "I corrected her.

"Oh, you're going by your street name now?"

"Nah, you just can't call me by my government."

"I remember when I could."

"Yeah, well not anymore. Being that I don't anticipate seeing you any time soon we don't have to worry about that now do we," I told her.

She gave me a smirk before walking out of my office. I hadn't digested the fact that she came here clearly on some bullshit before the door opened again.

"What the hell the witch doing here?" Russ asked.

"She claims her brother is looking to buy some land. I know she was here on some bullshit though."

"Yeah, I still don't trust her ass. She can't come to my house to feed my fish and I don't have any damn fish. I keep telling you that about her ass. She's too fucking sneaky for me. Are you thinking about fucking her again? I'm just asking," he said.

"Hell nah, I ain't got shit for her ass. She better go fuck her husband."

"That outside dick making her ass sick."

"It's been over a year if her ass was sick, she should be dead by now. What's up?"

"Have you talked to Grace? I wanna see how Mr. Geoff is doing," he said.

"Nah, who the fuck is Geoff? I haven't talked to her for few days," I said.

"Her uncle, he's Rick's pops. He had a heart attack or some shit. When I talked to Rick the day before yesterday he was up at the hospital. I hadn't heard from him but, I know you were trying to get close with Grace so I thought you would know something," he said.

I sent Grace a text asking her where she was and how was her uncle. She responded saying she was at the hospital but, never said how her uncle was doing. I took my keys off the desk and headed to the door. I didn't know what was going on but, I felt the need to be up there with her instead of calling her on the phone.

"Scarlet, I'm heading out for the rest of the day," I told my secretary.

I didn't know if she acknowledged what I said because I didn't wait around for her to respond. If she needed me for something, she would text me on my business line.

"I'm gonna follow you," Russ called out as I made it to my car.

I didn't pay him any mind either. If she was at the hospital with her family, why hadn't she mentioned it while we were texting for the past two days? We didn't have a long drawn out text conversation but, she didn't say shit about her uncle being sick or nothing. Just when I thought we were getting somewhere. Her and all these walls were gonna have to move around. We talked so she considered me a friend at the least. As her friend I was gonna come to her aid even though her head strong ass didn't feel like she need it. I understood that she didn't know how to lean on others but, she was damn sure gonna learn today.

Walking into the hospital the hairs on the back of my neck stood up. I hated these fucking places. I had never come to a hospital for anything good like the birth of a child. I know this was a place where people come when they get sick but, I had only come here when people were dying or damn near dead. Once you come to a place three or more times to only get some fucked up news your subconscious causes your body to react to that place automatically. Right now, I was feeling sick to my stomach.

"Grace," I called out to her when I walked into the waiting area.

Russ came up with the next elevator. I forgot that he said he was going to follow me due to my mind being on Grace right now. He stood next to me scoping out the crowd that was slowly getting larger in the waiting area.

"Wh-What are you doing here?"

"I just heard about your uncle. I came up here to be with you. You don't need to be alone right now. You should've told me what was going on but, we'll talk about that tomorrow."

"He had a heart attack two days ago. When he first got here, they did a surgery on him. He came out of that okay then out of nowhere late last night he had another heart attack. I don't know if I'm coming or going. You didn't have to come here to see about me. I know you're a busy man. I'm sure you have other shit to do," She told me.

I could feel everyone's eyes on me. My only concern right now was Grace. Just by looking at her I could tell she hasn't gotten any sleep. There were bags under her eyes that told their own story. I know if she hasn't slept then she probably hasn't eaten either.

"When is the last time you had something to eat?" I asked her.

"I had some chips and a half sandwich from the vending machine," she answered.

"So, you're not eating or sleeping how is that healthy for you. I know that you're worried about your uncle but, you're gonna make yourself sick."

"Grace, he's right you need to eat and try to get some rest," a man's voice said from behind me.

race

"Blaine what are you doing here?" I asked him.

Gully coming was somewhat understandable because he and I were getting close. Blaine, on the other hand had no business being here. He and I had no attachments to each other.

"How the hell he black and his name is Blaine?" Gully mumbled under his breath but, I heard him loud and clear.

"I came here for some testing and saw your car in the parking lot. I went to a few waiting areas before this one. I couldn't leave the hospital without knowing if you were okay," Blaine said.

There was no way what he just said could make any sense to him. He was sounding crazy to me and from the faces of everyone else in the room they agreed with me. What type of shit was he on?

"Stalking ass black motherfucker named Blaine," Gully said as he put his arm around my waist.

I knew he was making this statement to Blaine that he and I were more than friends. I didn't mind because Blaine had no business being here anyway. Hopefully, the presence of Gully will make him leave.

"I'm sorry I didn't catch your name or the reason why you're here," Blaine said to Gully.

"This isn't the time or place for any of this right now. Blaine you need to leave," I told him.

"Grace who is this guy? You didn't say anything about him when I saw you a couple of weeks ago," Blaine said making shit sound way more personal than it was.

"Don't do that Blaine. You last saw me at the grand opening don't start that shit. Look, thank you for coming to check on me but, I'm just fine physically," I told him.

I could feel Gully squeezing my side as I was talking. I was thinking that he was going to interject while I was talking. Thankfully he didn't I just needed Blaine to take his ass on.

"I find it funny that he wasn't close to you when that was one of the best nights of your life," Blaine said with a smirk.

"Oh, I was there trust me I came well, both of us did that night didn't we baby?" Gully said with a smirk on his face.

"Grace you deserve someone better than a man that discusses your sex life," Blaine said with his face showing how embarrassed he was by what Gully had said. Gully stepped in front of me so that he and Blaine were nose to nose.

"Judging by the extreme tightness of her; I know why you don't talk about your sex life. You ain't got shit to be proud about."

"Blaine can you just go?" I asked from over Gully's shoulder. I had tried to push him to the side, but he wasn't budging.

"Yeah, Blaine bounce," Gully said.

I hit Gully on his back but, he still didn't budge. I could see my Auntie GiGi and cousins looking trying to figure out what was really going on. I knew when Blaine left here, I was going to be bombarded with questions of who was who. Everyone in here probably thought I was gay before these two came in here acting like teenagers.

"I never thought you would end up with a thug."

"It's a good thing your thoughts don't count. I'm not a thug playboy. Put some respect on my motherfucking name."

"Grace call me when you have a chance to talk. I have something I would like to discuss with you," Blaine said as he started fidgeting with his suit jacket.

"Nah, if you didn't notice she's here with the entire family. You haven't even asked what everyone was here for. You keep adjusting that stiff ass Sears or JCPenney suit jacket but, it ain't gonna help the fit. Just leave while you're ahead. Don't reach out to her and she damn sure won't reach out to you. Take your ass on Braxton," Gully told him.

"Blaine, my name is Blaine," he told Gully with his chest poking out.

"Bye Braxton," Gully said as he pointed his finger in his chest. You could tell that Blaine was in pain just from the finger poking into his chest. If this wasn't a tense time right now, I would be laughing. "Don't put your hands on me."

"Oh yeah," Gully said with a smirk. Out of nowhere Gully smacked Blaine with an open hand.

My hand went over my mouth to keep from screaming.

"Yo, okay that's enough of this bullshit. Grace, I don't know if I should be proud or lay your ass out for having this fine nigga in here protecting your ass and shit. Steve, I need you to leave," My Auntie GiGi said.

"Steve? Who is Steve?" Blaine asked.

"You are due to the fact that you're looking like Steve Urkel and shit. Bye," she said looking at him sternly.

Blaine finally left and I finally felt some relief.

"Ma'am I'm sorry I had to act out like that. It was not my intention by coming here. I'm only here to make sure Grace is okay."

"I understand handsome. You've been all up in my niece's space since you been here. I doubt you even noticed there were other people here," Auntie GiGi said giving him a big smile.

She was laying it on thick right now. He was standing there smiling loving it up. It was borderline disgusting to watch her flirt with him like this.

"Family of Geoff Reynolds," a doctor came in dressed in full scrubs with a lab coat over them. We all rushed over to where he was.

"Yes, he's my brother," Auntie GiGi said.

"Mr. Reynolds had blockages in two of his arteries leading to the heart. We had to clear the blockages and inserted stents in those arteries. There weren't any complications with the surgery. He's still sleeping once the anesthesia wears off, he should be waking up. He's going to be in a lot of pain for the first two days but, that should lessen with time. We have him being moved into a room on the cardiac ICU wing. Once he gets settled in, we will allow two people at a time to visit with him."

"That doesn't sound safe for him to get visitors at this time. He's just had two open heart surgeries in three days. It just doesn't sound good to me," Rick said.

I agree with him the main thing that Uncle Geoff needs right now is rest. People going in and out of his room isn't going to help.

"We can work all that out later Ricky," Auntie GiGi told him.

"I'm just saying," he replied.

"Thank you so much for the update doctor."

Everyone was relieved by the news that the doctor had given us. Auntie GiGi went to call her brothers that were out of the country working to give them an update.

"You don't look too good," Gully told me. I started to say something to him then everything went black.

OOOOOO

I woke up with a headache, dry mouth and Gully staring at me with an unreadable look on his face.

"I'm gonna get the doctor," he said getting up and heading out of the door.

The vibe was off but, I wasn't feeling well enough to even address it right now. I just needed the doctor to come in and give me my discharge papers. I was going to check on Uncle Geoff then take my ass home to get some sleep. That was all that I needed some good old rest in my own bed. Gully came back in the room with a serious look on his face. The doctor walked in with a smile on his face.

"Nice to see your pretty eyes are open now," he said I heard Gully start coughing. I rolled my eyes at him. "Well you haven't been getting the proper amounts of rest and fluids for someone in your condition. Your blood pressure is extremely high. You need to get rest, fluids, and stay away from stress if you want to have a safe delivery," he said.

"Whoa hold up! Delivery of what?" I asked. He looked at Gully then back to me. "Oh, I thought he told you before I got in here. You're four weeks pregnant."

"Pregnant? You mean pregnant with a baby?"

"Yes, now in order to make it to the delivery you're going to have be on strict bedrest for the first two trimesters. I want to see that you know how to control your stress and how you control your reactions to the stress that's around you. I understand that you're a business owner, I would strongly suggest that you get an assistant or even two. Stress can cause you to lose the baby. This is very serious," he told me.

Gully was sitting there looking like he was ready to kill me and the doctor. The doctor asked if I had any more questions then he left. I was trying to get my thoughts together in my head when Gully started talking.

"If you go against the doctor's rules and lose my baby, I'm gonna fuck you up," he said.

"Well, that's very stressful for you to threaten me like that. Not only do I have to worry about what the hell to do with the lounge but, I have you threatening my life."

"Keep playing with me," he told me as he scooted the chair closer to the bed.

"I'm not playing. You don't just tell someone that you're gonna kill them and just go on with life like you just told me hi. Germain, I don't need all that on me right now."

"You're right that's why you're coming to stay with me," he told me.

I turned my head to look at him because I knew I had to have heard him wrong.

"I don't know you well enough to come stay with you," I told him.

"But you know me well enough to be carrying my child. You might as well get over that bullshit in your head. You're staying with me and that's it. I'm gonna make sure your hardheaded ass doesn't do anything to jeopardize my child making it here. If I have to tie your big head to the bed, then that's what I'll do. Go head and do the little attitude shit now because it's going down," he told me.

I just stared at him. He wasn't paying me no mind. He kicked his feet outstretched out, laid his head back and closed his eyes. Oh, he just knew that what he said was law.

CHAPTER 10

Gully

Grace really thought that her pouting all day was gonna change something. What her childish ass didn't know was that I had already cleared it with her whole family before I told her anything. When the doctor came in telling us what was going on with her, I told them all that she was gonna come to stay at the house with me. There weren't any objections but, she had two hoe ass cousins that were trying me. They could keep on and I was gonna have to hurt their feelings. I told Rick about them but, he just brushed it off telling me not to entertain them. I left it alone but, they weren't gonna be satisfied until I let them know that I wasn't family dick.

I wasn't planning on leaving her here before we found out she was pregnant. Now that I know my ass had been camped out right here in this hard ass chair. She was trying to give me the quiet treatment but, I didn't give a fuck if she talked to me as long as my child wasn't harmed in her attitude having episodes. She was gonna learn that rolling her eyes, mumbling under her breath, and slick ass comments didn't move me. I know just by how she's acting that she was always in charge in the relationship. Not to say that we were in a real relationship but, since she was having my first child, she was my responsibility. She could yell and scream all she wanted to. I wasn't here to make her comfortable I was here to make sure she followed the doctors' orders.

"Are you sure you don't want me to come over there to lay her ass out and get her in line?" Her Auntie GiGi asked me.

"No ma'am I got it. She can fight me all she wants as long as she's sitting her behind down somewhere," I told her causing her to laugh.

"That girl can give an order that's for sure. The problem comes in when she has to follow orders. We all made sure she was headstrong but, I think sometimes we did too good of a job with her."

"It's all good when she figures out I'm nothing like Urkel or those other boys that she's dealt with in the past everything will be just fine."

"I know about my skanky ass nieces trying to get at you. Just let me know when you need me to knock the shit out of them. I don't think they're my nieces any damn way. They act just like their hoe ass mama's. My brothers Gary and Geon were known for taking in strays," she said as she rolled her eyes.

It was funny how much she looked like Grace when she did that. I could tell that Grace had acquired a lot of her Auntie GiGi's mannerisms. I caught myself wondering if this was what I had to look forward to when Grace got older. There was so many similarities between the both of them.

"I need to give you my phone number," I told her, and her eyes got big.

"Now, you're fine and everything but, I'm not that kind of Auntie GiGi. You and your muscles will never experience the tightness of this vintage loving that I have. I could never hurt my niece like that. You know she's the only one that acts like the rest of us. That's why she's the only one I will ever claim in public."

"No, I was gonna give you my number so you could call me to check on your hardheaded niece."

"Oh yeah that makes sense. Just don't send me no unsolicited pictures of your body parts because I don't send them back," she said with a smile.

"You are a trip."

"All in fun young man. I would never cross those lines. We just need some laughter around here. You have my nephew upset and too scared to cry because they're men. My brothers stayed out of the country because they're avoiding the hospital like the plague. I have the thot twins here trying to figure out how the 'ice queen' snagged a nice looking hunk of meat like you. I'm the only one here that's normal. That's too much pressure for my old fine self to handle. Wait a minute what were we talking about?" She asked seriously.

"Don't even worry about it. Let me see your phone so I can put my number in it."

She handed it to me with a smile on her face.

"Make sure you put your name in there as my fine ass nephew in law."

I couldn't stop myself from laughing at her. She was seriously funny. This is the most I've laughed since I got to this damn place. Auntie GiGi was the breath of fresh air that I needed right now. I handed her the phone back she took it from me with a huge smile on her face. I could tell just by looking at her that she was a fine woman in her hay day. I was low-key wondering why she was single. Even for a woman in her sixties she still could pull a few old niggas that much I knew.

"Why are you still single Auntie GiGi?"

"Young man, don't you start asking me stuff just to see an old lady blush," she said tapping me on my shoulder.

"No ma'am, I'm not asking for any other reason than for you to clear up my confusion. I'm sure there's a deacon somewhere that needs you in their life."

"No, that love ship has sailed away many years ago. I'm not an old lady with a bunch of cats so don't worry yourself about me," she said then she walked away.

I turned around to see hoe and hoetta making their way to me. A few years ago, I would take them both up on the pussy they were trying to pass me. Now, not so much, I didn't even want to be seen talking to them without one of the other family members around. To add insult to injury they weren't even the type of hoes to keep a secret. I could tell they wanted some attention or interaction with me so they could go tell Grace. Granted I wasn't even thinking about giving them conversation and definitely hadn't thought about letting them see the dick, but they just had the 'tell all the other hoes' look to them.

"So how long have you been messing around with our cousin? Is you the baby's daddy for real?" One of them asked.

Just when I was about to say something to them my phone rang. *Look at God!*

"I gotta take this," I said as I walked away. "Hello," I said once I was far enough away for them not to hear me.

"You work quick as hell bruh. Did you do that shit on purpose? Let me find out you're out here trapping females and shit" Russ asked laughing.

"Is that all you called me for? Weren't you just here? When did you leave?"

"You seemed like you were good, so I left. So, what's the answer?"

"Yeah she is and it's mine."

"I never thought you would try to trap a female man. This is so disappointing."

"Trap a female, nah this ain't that. I admit I've never strapped up or pulled out but, I wasn't on some trap her shit. The shit just happened and now it is what it is. I wasn't thinking about making a baby but, now that it's coming, she better not try to kill my kid," I told him.

I was happy that the word abortion didn't come out of her mouth. Grace was one of those in control type of females, so I was low-key expecting her to say that word. She hasn't so far but, you never know with Grace.

"So, you never pulled out or strapped up. Did y'all even talk about birth control or diseases before you went up in her all sushi and shit?"

"Sushi, what the hell is that?"

"RAW nigga ain't that what Sushi is RAW FISH?"

"Only you would think that that analogy made sense. To answer your question though we didn't talk about shit."

"You never move like this what the fuck is up? You have a long list of hoes that you only fuck with if they come to you with a clean test but, with Grace you're doing shit ass backwards what gives?"

I understood where he was coming from because I had thought about the same thing while Grace was sleeping in her hospital bed. To add to the path of backwards movements here it is I was about to move her into my house *after* she was already pregnant. There wasn't a discussion of a relationship or if we had a future together. I guess the lord stepped in and gave us a baby to ensure that we had a future.

"I don't have an answer for you. Shit is just different with Grace. I knew she was going to be different just by how she was moving when we first met but, she was in a whole different league all together. Sometimes when I talk to her, I feel like I'm talking to myself. She doesn't move like other females out here. I basically had to tell her that she was going to my house when she got out of here. She still fought me on it even though she knows that it's best for them both that she goes to my house. Any other female out here would find out that she's pregnant with my baby and she would be ready to move in and spend my damn money. Grace doesn't want shit from me. She too used to handling shit on her own. It's gonna be more fighting once I get her to the house watch what I tell you."

"Damn it sounds like you have a problem on your hands. This should be interesting," Russ said laughing.

"Ain't shit funny man."

"Oh yes the hell it is. I'm here for you man. So, what are you gonna do because you know Grace is the type to climb out the window if you try to hold her hostage?"

"I'm gonna chain her ass to the bed," I told him seriously.

He didn't take me seriously because he was falling out on the phone laughing at me until the call ended. He could laugh all he wanted to but, I was dead ass. If she didn't cooperate with me, I was gonna have to chain her ass to the bed to make sure she didn't do too much and lose my damn baby. I know it sounded crazy but, shit crazy is the best way to describe my black ass.

race

"Grace that man cares about you. I had to make him go home and take a shower. He's been right here the entire time. I know you see it that he loves you. It's more behind how he feels than this pea sized baby you're carrying around. Don't mess this up. He may be good for you," Auntie GiGi told me.

I was getting tired of her sudden 'Go Gully' campaign. She came in here and asked me once how I felt. When I told her, I was fine considering the circumstances she shook her head and had been talking about Gully ever since. I don't know when or how they talked enough for her to be so ready for me to go live with him but, I still wasn't feeling the living situation.

"He doesn't care about me. The only thing he cares about is the child that I'm carrying. He has to take care of me because of the baby and that's it. Don't read too much into it. It's not like we're getting married and riding off into the sunset. This isn't a damn fairytale. I'm not the beauty even though his ass is the beast."

She just looked at me and shook her head.

"You young folks never want to listen to us older folks. I honestly don't understand how y'all need to learn things the hard way. That man cares about you more than you would ever care to notice. I see you giving that man nothing but a fight once you leave this hospital. You need to let go and let him take care of you. If my niece or nephew doesn't get here with all ten fingers and toes; I'm beating your ass once your six weeks are up. I know we raised you to be strong but, sometimes your best sign of strength is to know when to let others take the lead. I know you like I was the one to give birth to you my damn self. I know that you're going to use that damn phone to stay up to date on what you need to know about that lounge. Grace the doctors didn't come in here and put you on bed rest just because they felt like it. There is a reason for it, pay attention. If you try to sneak to get work done, I'll beat your ass with your granddaddy's cane," she fussed.

I didn't say anything because everything that I was thinking was surely going to get me popped in this hospital bed. It was crazy how violent she was but, she looked like a regular old lady that played bingo. The fact was that she could be more violent than my uncles. I knew by her tone that she was serious. I still didn't think that me moving in with Gully was a good idea. I guess none of this would be taking place if I didn't think fucking him with no protection was a good idea either. I was going to have to deal with my consequences. Unfortunately, the consequences consisted of me living with a man that I was deep in lust with and pregnant by. Maybe moving in with him wasn't bad at all.

"Auntie GiGi it looks like I don't have a choice."

"I knew that you didn't have a choice when he let all of us know what he planned to do while you were in here still in la-la land. I just want you to give it an honest try before you mess around and fuck up a good thing. Let the man take care of you and his child. Everything that he tells you is for the benefit of your child. As long as you remember that then you'll be fine. It's when you start thinking he's trying to control you is when the problems are going to start."

"Auntie GiGi, how do you know I'm going to think that?"

"Because I know you," she said shaking her head.

Gully walked in with some jeans and a t-shirt on with some Jordan's on his feet. This was my first time seeing him dressed down. All the other times I've seen him he was dressed for a business meeting. I never knew that jeans could be so damn sexy on a man. The shirt was short sleeved, so his tattoos were on full display. Those strong arms of his were clouding my judgement right now something terrible. I wanted to feel them wrapped around me while he did whatever he wanted with my body. How was it when I look at him, I instantly wanted to feel him inside me?

"How are you feeling today?" He asked me.

"I'm doing okay. I want to get out of here though."

"Hey, nephew how are you doing? I'm just here keeping her company until you got here. If I'm here with her she won't try to escape," she said laughing.

She was laughing but, there wasn't nothing funny about what she said. I was really trying to plan an escape last night while Gully was sleeping. His phone rang as he sat down. He looked at it and slid it back in his pocket. I had to bite my lip to keep from asking him who it was that he just ignored. I know I had no business feeling like I could ask him anything but, I really wanted to.

"I'm chilling Auntie GiGi. Grace, if you have a question just ask it."

"I'm gonna get out of here so I can rest these old bones. Take care of my family Gully."

Once the door closed Gully turned to look at me. I know he

was waiting on me to ask him about the phone call but, he was going to be waiting until Jesus came back. I wasn't asking him anything. We weren't together we just happen to be having a child together.

"How can we get to know each other before the baby comes if you keep holding your tongue? There ain't shit you can't ask me. Holding your tongue can be a form of stress. The best way to live stress free is to say what's on your mind."

"I have no claims to you I can't question you about the calls you're ducking."

"You can question me about anything you want as long as my baby gets here healthy. Are you ready for the answer? What if the answer is something that's going to make you upset? Then what am I supposed to do then?" He asked.

I understood what he was saying but, we were going to have to come to some kind of agreement.

"Look I know you're not out here being celibate, and I would never expect you to be. There wasn't a relationship established when we started having casual sex and I'm not gullible enough to think that you want to be in one now that I'm pregnant. Me going to your house is nothing more than you taking care of our kid," I told him.

"I'm gonna wear your independent ass down soon enough."

"Is that what I am to you a challenge that you need to conquer? Let me guess, you and your friends made a bet about how far you will get with me. How much was the pay off?" I asked him.

Before I could close my mouth, he was up and in my face with a look that I've never seen before.

"I know you're just talking shit right now. That's the only reason I'm not gonna choke the shit out of you in the most loving way possible right now. Check this out though the next time you accuse me of some fuck boy shit like that I'm gonna fuck you so good that you're gonna be dreaming of the next time we fuck before I finish. One thing you'll learn about me is I'm not a kiss and tell kind of nigga. That's some gay ass shit. Don't fucking disrespect me like that again. Think about the shit you say before you say it next time."

He walked out of the room. I knew I had crossed a line but, I couldn't stop myself from talking. My heart was beating fast as hell. I had to start taking deep breaths hoping that would calm me down.

"Cuz what you do to ya boy? He's outside in the parking lot smoking and walking," Rick asked with a chuckle.

"I said some shit I shouldn't have said."

"When are you gonna let go and let his ass lead?"

"Lead what? We're not in a relationship," I said rolling my eyes.

"Cuz, I hate to be the bearer of bad news but, this nigga is moving you in his house. I bet he ain't tell you while you're in here he has a whole work crew getting the house ready for you. Your clothes and shit are already at his place, your room is set up and everything. You might not be in a relationship but, that nigga ain't playing about you or the baby your carrying. You're the holdup cuz, just like always. It's time for a change man."

I thought about what Rick was saying. Maybe I did need to start easing up a little bit. I just don't know how. Letting anyone besides family in wasn't something that I did. Even with family there were only a select few that knew anything about me. They could all get together and talk about what they knew but, that still wouldn't amount to much. Letting people in wasn't my thing.

"How can I change? I've been like this all my life," I told him.

"I don't have the answer to that. Maybe you need to just do the opposite of your first mind. Since your mind is all fucked up.

You gotta try cuz for real. I see Gully just might be the one to break your ass down," he told me with a smile on his face.

"Why do men always want to break a woman down? What is it about having control of a woman that makes men feel more important?"

"See that's what's wrong with most of y'all women. It's not about control shit if a nigga is telling you what to wear, who to hang out with, how to talk, changing how you interact with your family all of that is some control shit. All a real man wants is the proper respect and to feel that he's needed by his woman. I'm not saying needed in the sense of taking care of her either. Just like a man needs a woman to be his peace, his motivation and all that other good shit that's what Gully wants from you. You're too busy trying to fight him on everything to see that he's only being the man, the real man that you need to compliment and elevate you. Get ya shit together Grace. I usually don't get in your shit but, that nigga is worth the changes that you need to make. Just think about it. I love ya cuz," Rick told me as he kissed my forehead and left my room.

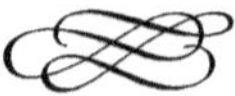

CHAPTER 12

*G*ully

I don't know how long I had been out here walking and smoking trying to calm down enough to go sit in there with Grace. I know I had to have patience with her but, she was killing me today. It hurt me that she automatically classified me with those fuck niggas that she had been dealing with. I'm not gonna lie there was a time when I was that nigga but, nah not with her. My trigger finger was itching to kill every nigga that had hurt her to the point to where she was skeptical of every nigga. I know for a fact that the nerd had something to do with how her mind worked.

"Aye Gully," Rick called to me as he walked up on me. I hope he's not on some bullshit because he damn sure can get the ass kicking his cousin needed.

"What's up?"

"I need you to have the patience of Babyface when dealing with Grace and her issues. She didn't tell me anything about what made you come out here pacing and shit. I just know her. Why do you think we call her the Ice Queen? I know she said some shit that has you out here trying to calm down. I'm gonna tell you just like I told her. I think you're good for her. The more she pushes the more you have to show her you're not going anywhere. That's what she needs."

I stood there trying to digest what he was saying. I know he was telling the truth. If she was gonna keep saying shit out of the side of her neck I was gonna end up choking the snot out of her fine ass.

"Since she's carrying my lil man she's gonna have to do way more than talk to me crazy for me to leave her. I'm only out here because I didn't want to do or say something that I know I'll regret later. I can tell she's used to saying stupid shit and people walking away from her. I ain't on that type of time with her," I told him.

The nigga looked like he was relieved that I wasn't gonna let her run me away. The shit made me laugh at his ass.

"Why you look like you're all relieved and shit?"

"Man, shit, because I am. Grace was destined to be a lonely old hag before you came along to shake her ass up. Stay away from the thot twins too," he added with a chuckle.

This nigga was always laughing at some shit. I didn't think he noticed them two eye fucking me. I didn't care if they all peeped it, they were disrespectful as fuck to be acting like that knowing I was with Grace and with their uncle in the damn hospital. Some chicks just didn't have any home training.

"Is there anything that you don't laugh about?"

"Yeah, folks fucking with my family, ain't shit funny about that. You're more family than they are."

"That's the same thing your aunt said. What the fuck is up with that?"

"Back in the day Uncle Geon and Gary were dating two cousins. The cousins were some straight up hoes but, they didn't care. They came to my grandparents' house talking about they were pregnant. Auntie GiGi wanted to fight both of them because she swears, they were putting some other niggas kids on her brothers. The uncles told her to chill when the girls were born, they got blood tests that said they were the fathers. Even though Auntie GiGi looked at the paperwork she still says they aren't Reynolds just because of how loose they are. They didn't come around much because Auntie GiGi ain't wrapped too tight and was trying to fight the mothers every time they came around. Now that the girls are older Auntie GiGi just tolerates them. She lets them know that she's just tolerating them though," he laughed.

I shook my head because I could see her old ass telling them that shit. She was a damn trip that's for sure.

"Let me go back up here with her. You be safe out here," I told him. We dapped each other up and I took a deep breath and headed back up to the room with the mother of my child. When I got to the door there was a bunch of laughing going on. Walking in the room I saw a dark-skinned chic with tears in her eyes from laughing so much. I remembered seeing her at the lounge for a few minutes at the grand opening.

"Well damn bitch, do he have a brother?" She said loud as hell.

"Gully this is my best friend Adrian. Adrian this is …"

"Your sexy ass baby daddy. I see why you busted open for him."

"Can you be any more embarrassing? Don't pay her no mind. It takes time to get used to her she doesn't mean any harm," Grace said looking nervous.

"It's all good. Nice to meet you," I said as I sat down.

"Thank you for coming into my friend's life. She's been needing to get a life for a long time now. Let's get to the nitty gritty. Do you have a bunch of hoes? You look like one of those niggas that walk into a room and chics just get naked hoping to be chosen by you."

Oh, this chic was funny as hell.

"I don't have time for hoes. My only concern is making sure my baby gets here healthy. Everything else doesn't mean shit to me. I got her and everything else."

Adrian started fanning herself and looking around like someone else was in the room.

"Grace, bihhh if you don't lock this man down, I know something. You're good in my book bestie-in-law. Be easy with my friend here she's smart as hell book and business wise. When it comes to relationships and matters of the heart you would think she was riding the short bus to school with a helmet on and licking the windows," she said seriously.

I couldn't do anything but laugh at her. She was worse than Auntie GiGi. How could they be so off the hook but, Grace was being a difficult ass broad? She was the only one who barely smiled and thought way too long about what she said and did. Hopefully I could change that up sooner than later.

"Yo nigga, let me holler at you for a minute. Hey Grace, good to see you sitting up and shit. Congratulations on the baby," Russ said as he kissed Grace on the forehead. He stopped what he was doing when he noticed Adrian. He looked like he was stuck, and she was looking a little pissed. She wasn't laughing or smiling like she was a few minutes ago.

"Yo! Russ! What the fuck?" I said to get his attention they were just staring at each other and shit. He turned and walked the fuck out. When I made it out of the door, he was standing facing the wall with this forehead pressed against it. "What was that?" He took a deep breath then turned to face me.

"I came to give you Grace's keys to her car and house. All her clothes and shit have been moved. The nursery is almost done, the fridge is stocked, new appliances and gadgets and shit in the kitchen. The surveillance system is getting installed in the morning."

He was talking to me but, I could tell his mind was somewhere else. I nodded my head but, was wondering what the hell was going on with him. He seemed rattled about seeing old girl but, shit I could be wrong.

"Thanks for making sure shit is taken care of at the house for me," I told him.

"I ain't doing the shit for your ugly ass, I have to make sure my niece or nephew get a good start when they get here. If you and Grace keep beefing like you have been the baby's gonna look just like your ugly ass. It's all good though I'll teach the kid how to fight," he said with a forced smile.

I could've asked him what was going on again but, his ass heard me the first time. If he wanted me to know then he would tell me. I had my own shit to worry about. He left and I went back in the room. The girl Adrian was still looking shook.

"Are you okay?" I asked her. She didn't answer. When I looked at Grace she was looking just as concerned about her friend as I was about Russ right now.

"Friend I love you but, I'm gonna leave. I'll call you later on tonight."

Grace and I watched as she left.

"What the hell was that about?" Grace asked me.

"I don't know Russ ain't answer my ass either. Whatever it is they are two grown ass people they'll work it out."

"I hope so. I haven't seen her mad like that in a long time. It doesn't make sense though because they didn't say anything to each other," Grace said.

"Don't think about it too hard. That ain't good for my kid or for you. How have you been feeling?" I asked.

"I'm fine just bored. I know you have other shit you could be doing instead of sitting up here with me. I'm ready to go home. I need to sleep in my own bed."

I just listened to her talk. I knew I needed to save my energy for when she did get released. I know I told her she was coming to my house so there shouldn't be an argument there. The argument was gonna come in when she finds out that I packed up her place and changed the locks.

CHAPTER 13

Russ

Mother fucking Adrian, of all the times before I had been looking for her and never seen her. I walk in a hospital room and there she is bold as fuck. I could've snapped her fucking neck. I still might but, I need answers first. I stood beside the elevator doors that led to the parking garage of the hospital waiting for her ass to come out. If I knew her like I thought I did her ass was going to leave after me to get a head start on getting away from me. Her fucking time running was done. I stood there thinking about the day my heart and world shattered. I hadn't heard from Adrian for a few days. Her moms didn't like me because I was a 'drug dealing nigga' and she felt like I was a little too old for Adrian at the time. She stayed trying to tell Adrian that I was cheating or some other bullshit to try to get her to break up with me.

Pulling up to Adrian's mom's house I felt weird as hell. I should've known that shit wasn't good. Adrian and I talked to each other every day and here it was going on day four that she wasn't picking up for me or returning my phone calls. I rang the doorbell and her mom came to the door with a cigarette hanging out of her mouth.

"What the fuck you want?" She asked.

"Is Adrian here?"

"Oh, you want to talk to my daughter so you can spoil her some more? Well, guess what she ain't gonna be one of the many for your thugnificiant ass. She got that drug dealing baby sucked out and she's gone. I told her to never come back. She has her whole life ahead of her. She won't be another black girl lost not on my watch. So, go on and forget about her she was too young for your ass anyway."

She just stood there like she didn't just take my heart out and step on it. Adrian was my lil baby that no one knew about. I kept her tucked away not because I was ashamed or embarrassed. The only people that knew about her were the people closest to me. Gully was living in New York at the time, so he never met Adrian. Whenever I talked about him to her, I always called her my girl. He always joked that she was invisible or some shit. The streets and street niggas never played fair. I kept her tucked away for her own good. I did it because I loved her.

I still thought about her ass to this day and that was years ago. I had two pictures of us at my main house now hanging up. I don't stay in that house much because it's too big. That was the house that Adrian and the baby were supposed to move into. No one but me, the realtor, and the moving company knew about that house. I had thought of selling it over the years but, I couldn't bring myself to do it. Somewhere in the back of my mind and heart I always hoped she would come back. If I would've sold the house that meant I was giving up on her coming back to me.

I shook my head thinking about how mad she looked when she saw me. I don't know what the fuck she was pissed about. Her ass was the one that fucking disappeared. The dinging of the elevator brought me back to my fucked up reality. Her mind was so gone that she didn't even pay me any mind as she fast walked to her car. I was right behind her the entire time not once did she think to look behind her. That pissed me off because I always told her to be aware of her damn surroundings.

"You're still not fucking paying attention to your surroundings," I said making her stop. I was waiting for her to turn around but, she never did. "You picked up and left without a word to me and you still can't look me in the damn face. Come on man, you're starting to piss me off all over again. I know you hear me lil' baby," I told her.

She just didn't know I could stand here and talk to her back all damn day. It wasn't going to make me a fucking difference. She wasn't leaving out of my sight before she talked to me and explained why the hell she left like she did.

"Russell I can't do this with you right now."

"Too fucking bad because, you're not leaving until we get some shit settled."

"I figured you would just forget about me eventually. I was just a seventeen year-old in high school. I'm sure there were woman that were more of a match for you."

"More of a match for me; why because they were older? They were also the same gold digging, clout chasing, dick riding, and drug dealer hopping hoes they always were. You weren't like that though. I didn't have to worry if you were setting a nigga up or trying to trap my ass. Yeah, you got knocked up anyway but, that was more my fault than it was yours. TURN THE FUCK AROUND AND LOOK AT ME! Look at me and tell me you aborted my child and our relationship at the same time. You never even fucking called. I had to go to your mom's house and let that bitch tell me."

I was so fucking angry. It felt like the shit had happened yesterday instead of years ago. Adrian had no idea how much I loved her. She was the one to fuck my head up. A fucking teenager broke my damn heart. I know I was dead wrong for dealing with her in the first place. I always wondered if the police would come knocking on my door. The way her mom broadcasted her hate for me but, she never called the police on my ass didn't make any sense to me. She finally turned to look at me. Her eyes were full of tears cascading down her beautiful chocolate skin.

"I left because I had to. She came to my mother's house saying how she was going to call the police on you for getting me pregnant. When she left my mom convinced me that you had her come over to tell me all that. Why would an older woman take time out of her day to lie about you to my young ass?"

She was so emotional, and I didn't have a clue of who or what the hell she was talking about. I can admit that there were a few women that I dipped in before I was into it heavy with Adrian but, I didn't tell nobody no shit like that. Didn't many people even know about her.

"Who are you talking about? Who came to your mom's house? Help me understand what you're talking about. I'm fucking lost. The only people that knew about you were the closest ones to me. None of them would tell you no bullshit like that," I told her.

"Caretha." (pronounced Care-Retha)

I never expected to hear that name. She couldn't be lying because Caretha and I started kicking it heavier than usual around that time. I wanted to kill that bitch. *How the fuck did she find out about Adrian though?*

"Give me your phone." I told her. She handed me her phone, I put my number in it and handed it back to her. "Answer when I call you later."

"What if I'm home with my boyfriend?" She had the nerve to ask.

"Tell that nigga to pack his shit and dip. Daddy's back and claiming everything that belongs to him and you're on the top of the list. Don't play with me and not answer the fucking phone Adrian," I said giving her a kiss.

I wanted to take her with me back to the house and catch up and all that other sappy shit but, I had a neck to wrap my hands around first. I couldn't drive fast enough to get to Caretha. Caretha's scandalous ass had been rocking with me for years. She was bitching and moaning about getting married and shit but, that wasn't happening. I wasn't marrying her. I couldn't put my hands on why I refused to marry her but, I could feel that she was on some other shit. After Adrian left, I never let another female in. Like I said she was young but, she was the one that had my heart. Even after all this time she was it for me.

I pulled up at Caretha's apartment building. I was so pissed that I don't remember touching all the steps on the stairs to get to her door on the third floor. I used the key I had to walk in. She came down the hallway with a smile on her face.

"Hey baby."

"I have a question to ask you and I need you to tell me the truth. I already know the answer just to warn you. Did you go to Adrian's house and tell her some bullshit about the police and her being pregnant?" I asked.

"Baby, you have to understand," she tried to explain.

"Yes or no!"

"I did it because you didn't need her. She was a fucking little girl. You needed a woman."

My hand was around her neck so fast that she didn't see it coming. Her hands were clawing at mine. Those small ass hands weren't a match for my large ones or the anger that I had in me at the time. She let her jealousy show for a woman that she swore was beneath her. Her going to the measures that she had gone to by going to her house showed me just how threatened she was when it came to Adrian. I don't blame her one bit. After Adrian dropped off the face of the earth, I was all fucked up. Caretha' sneaky ass was there to help me pick up the pieces the best way that she could. I was grateful for that until now finding that she's the reason for all the pain that I was in sent me over the edge. When I realized that her ass was about to check out, I abruptly removed my hands from her neck making her drop to the floor. I looked at her with disgust as she struggled to get her breathing together.

"You scandalous bitch. I thought you were helping me because you cared. The only reason why you helped me back then was because the shit was your fucking fault. She killed my damn child behind your lies. Then you were acting like you were a hero or some shit. I can't believe you. How the fuck did you find out about her and where the hell her mom's house was?"

"Russ you sleep like a fucking rock when I put it on you the right way. One night after I put you to sleep, I went through your phone to find out what was stopping you from committing to me. You started pulling back from me. We had gone from fucking on the regular to you just getting head from me. I knew it was something that caused you to switch up on me. I was hurt beyond belief when I saw it was a damn kid keeping us from being the family that we were meant to be."

"It was never a plan to be a family with you. Where the hell did you get that shit from. I wore two fucking rubbers with you but, you put it in your head that we were supposed to be a family," I said shaking my head. It was wild how these females were showing me how wrong they were for me while they were trying to convince me that we belong together.

"She wasn't right for you. I'm the one that's supposed to be your wife. Fuck that little bitch," she spat as she sat up on the floor.

"You did all that so I would marry your ass. How the fuck did that turn out for you? You conniving bitch you really thought that was gonna change anything. I should put your head through the damn wall."

"That young girl didn't know shit about taking care of a grown man the right way. She would've never lasted being wifey like I am right now. We've been through hell and high water, I'm still your woman!" She yelled.

"Woman? Who the fuck told you that you were my woman? When did I walk my ass in here and tell you that it was just gonna be me and you? If you were my woman, why is it when you see me out in the street with other women your ass is all hush mouthed. There's been plenty of occasions where I was with someone else at the same party, mall, concert, or whatever and you never once said anything to me about it."

"Those others never mattered. You were never gonna leave me so there was no need to even pay them any mind," she said with pride.

I shook my head at how stupid she sounded. This shit was unbelievable. How the hell is she saying she's fine with me going out with other women? She hasn't even asked if I was fucking them.

"I fucked them chics you know that right?" I asked.

"Russ none of that matters to me. I know I'm your main chic, so we don't need to discuss them."

"You're really okay with me fucking other chics?"

"Russ why must we talk about this? You want to know how I feel about it then I'll tell you. I don't care if you go out here and entertain other women. You're a man so being faithful isn't to be expected. I never approached you those times I saw you because I knew if I did that would cause unnecessary problems between you and me. I'm not going anywhere, and neither are you."

"Yes I am."

"What? What do you mean yes you are? You are what?"

"I'm leaving you alone and them other hoes too. You need to find you some worth or something because that shit you just said was the saddest shit I ever heard. You're worse than the women out here that are satisfied with having a piece of a man. You don't realize that you're single as fuck just like I am. I would never want my daughter to say some shit like that," I shook my head.

I never thought about how she felt about the situation we were in. Now hearing this shit only pissed me off because she ran Adrian away just to play on the team of bitches I've had for all these years. I started laughing once I thought about it.

"What's funny?"

"You are. You're fine with me being with other women but, you went out of your way to tear Adrian and I apart. Sitting around here talking about you're wifey. I'm gonna tell you now stay the fuck away from Adrian. She's gonna be what she was supposed to be before your messy ass went to her house."

"What was she supposed to be Russ?"

"Adrian will be my wife legally and the mother of my children, that's what."

I got up to leave out of her apartment and her life. I could hear her calling my name. I didn't care though. I only cared about getting back right with Adrian.

CHAPTER 14

$\mathcal{A}$drian

I had downed two bottles of wine since I left the hospital. I was trying to avoid feeling the pain that was slowly creeping up. When he walked into the room my heart exploded. Once it registered that he was standing there in real life the anger came. How could he be out here living life looking all sexy and shit? He had let his hair grow out and he had a beard. Oddly enough the combination didn't make him look like a caveman. He was still built like he was still in the gym three days a week. Standing six feet four chocolate skin with more tattoos than I remembered him having. He was still sporting the sexy smile that only enhanced the sexiness of his beard. Russell had eyes the color of amber. Skin that was smooth as freshly whipped butter. I wanted to run my hands through his hair and that thought popping in my head only pissed me off more. This man had taken my virginity, impregnated me, and broke my heart. I had no business thinking about how sexy he looked.

"I'm ready to give myself to you," I told him as we sat on his couch looking at TV.

"Nah, you don't have to do that. I told you already we can wait. I'm not trying to fuck your mind up. We're just vibing right now."

I felt my heart crack. I should've known that he was looking out for me but, I was seventeen and all I heard was that he didn't want me. That wasn't what he was saying but, that's still what I heard.

"Adrian don't look like that lil mama. I'm looking out. You're graduating soon so you need to concentrate on that not sex. I'm not going anywhere believe that."

"Okay," I said trying to hold back the tears. They fell anyway.

I felt so unwanted at that moment. My mom only wanted me around for my dad's child support. My dad paid child support, so he figured that made him being there physically, emotionally, and mentally optional. At the time the only thing I had on my side was Grace, and Russell. Auntie GiGi and I weren't as close as we are now at the time. I didn't feel comfortable discussing Russ with her back then. My life was different and then with the age difference between Russ and I stopped me from bringing it up with her or anyone else. During that time Grace and I were best friends but, I chose to keep what was going on at my house and with Russell to myself. There's no way Grace would understand how I feel and what I deal with. She had her whole family to be close to and to protect her. Until my mom found out about Russ ell and I getting close I might as well had been a piece of furniture. She never paid me any mind. I was lucky that she kept food in the house for me to eat.

"Shit Adrian don't cry baby," he told me.

He pulled me over to him so that I was sitting on his lap. He just let me cry that night. The next morning, he took me to get my nails and hair done. Instead of going to his place we ended up in a penthouse suite of one of the hotels on the Virginia Beach Oceanfront. The balcony was overlooking the water. He had candles set up all around the room. It was the most beautiful site that my young eyes have ever seen. I felt him wrap his arms around me after he closed the door.

"You deserve the world. If you're still ready, then we can do that tonight. I never want you to feel unwanted or unloved in my presence. I'm

prepared to take my time with you and show you what love is tonight. What do you think about that?" He asked me.

My mother was somewhere out in the streets, so I wasn't worried about going home anytime soon. I could probably stay here all week before she realized that I wasn't there with her. She never cared about my whereabouts as long as I stayed out of her way.

"Wow."

"Come on in here so you can take your bath. The water is already ran you can check to see if it's just the right temperature for you."

"You ran the water already? How when you were with me?"

"Don't worry about all that," he said as he scooped me up in his arms.

As he carried me to the bathroom, he was kissing me on my cheek and neck. My body was feeling things that I've never felt before. He placed me down on my feet. Before he helped me out of my clothes, he kissed me with so much passion that my head started to spin. Once all my clothes were off, he took my hand to help me get in the jacuzzi tub. I didn't get a chance to check the water, but it was perfect. He started taking his clothes off after I got settled.

"You're taking your clothes off too?"

"How else am I gonna bathe my baby? I made sure there was enough room for both us. It's all about you tonight. Just relax and let shit happen naturally." He stepped in with me. I had the biggest smile on my face this is the type of stuff I read about in books. I never thought a man catering to a woman was a reality. "What are you smiling for?"

"This is so awesome Russell."

"I just want you to chill out and do whatever you feel like doing. If you think you can't do this all the way just tell me to stop and I will. We can go get some chips and shit and chill out," he told me.

Just looking at him made me want to kiss him. That's exactly what I did. I put my hands on both sides of his face and kissed him with all I had in me. The kiss was so good that we both were moaning and grinding on each other. I could feel his hard dick bumping against my thighs and in between my legs.

"Put it in Russell," I pleaded.

"Nah man I can't take ya shit right here we supposed to be taking a bath."

"Russell please make love to me right now," I continued to beg.

"Damn it Adrian," he said as he wrapped his arms around me. "If it starts to hurt too much tell me and I'll stop," he said. I nodded my head up and down. I was too nervous, scared, excited, and horny to form any more words right now. My heart was beating fast with the anticipation of becoming a woman. It was a good thing that the jacuzzi was so big. He separated my legs. I could feel his dick touching the skin of my outer lips. He kissed me as he pushed himself inside of me. I yelled into his mouth but, never stopped the kiss. My eyes were shut tight as if that would ease the pain. He slowly slid out of me then back in at an even slower pace. When I opened my eyes, he was looking at me with his bottom lip trapped between his teeth. I don't know how many strokes it took for me to feel comfortable enough to start meeting his movements but, as soon as I did, he started cursing.

"Rus.. Russell what the .." I called out.

"Let it go my baby. Shit, I can't hold it no more," he said but it sounded like he was growling.

Two strokes later by body took over doing things like shaking, tingling, and making goosebumps as I experienced my first orgasm. He leaned over on to me trapping me between him and the wall. The feeling of his labored breaths against my wet skin tickled.

"I love you Adrian. I know it sounds crazy coming from me but, you had my heart before all of this. Being able to become one with you just sealed the deal for me. No one else will be able to have my heart unless you give it to them. You have it with you now until the end of time. That's never gonna change no matter what happens with us. I can promise you that."

That night was everything to me and I thought it was everything to him as well. It wasn't until five months after that that I found out I was pregnant. I was on top of the world that day. Speaking with him about everything we had it all planned out to the tee. I was gonna move in with him after graduation and everything. It wasn't until Caretha knocked on my mother's door that I was hit with the reality that I was just a child that he sold dreams to. After that day my life was never the same. I've had situations with other guys over the years. I just never took any of them seriously. I was always waiting for the ball to drop. The girlfriend that I didn't know about or the secret that they were keeping from me. I can say that although I was never fully vested in any of the relationships there was a part of me hoping and wishing that I would be enough for whoever the guy was at the time. Just as I suspected there was always something that tore us apart completely eventually.

I eventually stopped thinking that love was going to come to me. It became painfully clear that love wasn't in the cards for me. Love would never be an emotion that I would have the pleasure of feeling. In some ways I knew that it was because I was closed off to the men. It was always a matter of time they went looking for the affections that they weren't getting from me. Even knowing that I had a hand in every situation that dissolved; I was never motivated to allow myself to become so vulnerable to where I could feel the pain that Russell had given to me. That was a pain that I vowed to never feel again.

Getting up from the couch I had been sitting on since I came in the house, I went to the kitchen to get my last bottle of wine. The wine would make me sleepy enough for me to fall asleep. Before I could get everything into the room where I was going to spend the rest of my night my phone chimed letting me know I had a message.

757-667-0998: Adrian we have to sit down and talk about everything. I don't care when or where. I'm not letting you walk out of my life again. I know it's gonna take time for you to even sit down with me but, just know that I'm never gonna stop waiting for you. I haven't in all these years. How could I love another when the woman that held my heart and every-thing that I am has been so far away from me? I LOVE YOU ADRIAN!!!! Remember that shit.

After seeing that message I didn't want wine. I didn't want anything but to lay in my bed and cry about what could've been. Just when I was fine with never feeling love again here this motherfucker comes. This can't be life right now.

ully

Adrian had come to sit with Grace so that gave me a chance to slip out and go to the office. I needed to check on things with my own eyes. I hadn't been in the office since I found out Grace's uncle was in the hospital. Russ being my partner he knew how to run the office if I wasn't there but, I wasn't the type to just slack off. I first hit his office before going to mine to pick up some paperwork.

"What up?" I said walking in his office.

His office was the same size as mine. They were damn near identical except for the white leather chairs and sofa he had in here. The desk was a dark oak wood handcrafted one with a matching bar tucked in the corner. Russ had always said that the white leather gave his office a different ambiance than mine. I admit that it did. It was reflective of his laid back personality. I was more business oriented and borderline OCD with how I functioned in the office. Russ still got shit done and knew just as much shit about the business as I did. Our personalities were different but, we complimented each other in everything that we did that's why I trust him with my life above anyone else.

"What the hell you doing here? Who's at the hospital with Grace?" He asked.

"Damn, nigga, Adrian is there with her. I would rather run some errands than sit there and listen to them talk. What's going on with you and her?"

I was trying to let whatever they had going on happen naturally but the way they acted when they saw each other had me wanting to know what the deal was.

"When I find out what's up with us, I'll let you know."

I never seen my homie look as lost as he was right now. Whatever it was that was going on with them I knew that he would come talk to me when he was ready.

"Okay cool. How's everything going?"

"Everything is straight. I need your signature on a few things. I left you a stack in your office. I do want to know why Martina has been bringing her scallywag ass up here looking for you," he said giving me the side eye.

"Don't look at me like that. She says she wants me to help her brother buy some land. I already told her that I'm not doing it, so your guess is as good as mine as to why she's still trying. She can come looking all she wants but, I ain't helping her do shit," I told him.

"You know sis ain't gonna like that shit when she finds out Martina's sniffing around you again. You better fix that shit quick. Sis doesn't need a bunch of bullshit. I'm trying to be the uncle of the decade."

"Sis? Nigga how you gonna call her sis and we not even together for real?"

"Since y'all not together you won't mind a nigga taking her out and shit."

I kept my mouth closed because I knew his ass was just trying to get me started up. I wasn't about to start a back and forth thing with him. He just wanted me to get worked up with the thought of Grace getting with another man. I wasn't doing that with him because there wasn't gonna be another man in her life unless our child was a boy. Russ could kiss my ass for even talking about her with another man. I left out of his office with him laughing at me. I wasn't concerned about him right now. I got to my office signed the paperwork that he was talking about and started going through it.

"Mr. Spratley, I didn't know you were coming in today," Scarlet asked.

"I'm just here to put my signature on things where it's needed. I want to let you know that I appreciate you holding down the office while I've been dealing with some personal stuff."

"It's no problem. You remind me so much of son. It helps me by working here. If I didn't come to work, I would be home driving myself into a deep depression. It's my pleasure."

She walked out with a smile on her face. Scarlet wasn't much older than my mother. She didn't know that she was helping me by being here. My mother stayed on the west coast, so I didn't get to see her much. I talked to her a few times a week but there were days that I still missed her. Scarlet being here helped keep the days of missing her at bay.

Scarlet's son died in battle in Afghanistan a few years back. She was already working here when it happened. I never witnessed the pure strength of a black woman like I had during that time. My mother was strong but, Scarlet was on another level during that time. She got a visit from a military Chaplin and two service members here at the office. I was so pissed that they felt the need to tell her some news like that while she was working. I thought they had to wait until the person was home or something. Once she got together enough to go home, I dropped her off myself. I offered her to take a month off with pay but, she refused. She was out of work for a total of four days including the day of the funeral service. She knew that if she ever needed anything, I would be there for her no matter what it was. Scarlet was more than a secretary even if she didn't know it.

I signed the paperwork, returned a few phone calls then left the office. I know that Grace would want a nasty ass drink from Starbucks, so I stopped there to pick her one up on the way. Standing in line I heard Martina talking on her phone behind me. I don't know if she was next in line or if there were a number of people between us. She hadn't noticed me yet but, I knew it was only a matter of time. I took the cup of nasty drink off the counter. I hated that they called your name because when they called out the name Germain she stopped talking. I'm not in the mood to deal with her right now. Just hearing her voice put me in a bad mood most of the time.

"Gully, I was just on my way to your office," she said following me out of the door.

"Go away Martina. We don't have shit to talk about. Stop coming to the office too by the way."

"You're not going to stop and give me a face to face conversation?" she whined. I shook my head because she would always try that whining shit when she didn't get her way. It only made me want to slap the shit out of her. She was usually whining to try to get me to stay at her house or take her out on a date. She was the main pussy but, she wasn't satisfied and wanted a relationship that she didn't deserve or that I was ready for. I don't know if it was me or her that turned me off from making her my woman but, I knew then like I know now it will never work for us. She seemed to always forget that her ass was already married when it came to us. I thought that she had learned that but, I see now she was on some bullshit.

"We don't have shit to talk about. You want my help and I ain't helping."

I never bothered to face her, I said what I had to say and got in my car. She was standing there looking at my SUV's tail lights. She was some drama that I didn't need in my life right now. I pushed the thoughts of her out of my mind by the time I pulled into the parking lot of the hospital. When I walked into the room the doctor was laying some papers on the tray that was over the bed.

"I was just telling Ms. Reynolds that she doesn't have to go home but she has to get out of here," the doctor said laughing at his own joke.

"How long is it going to take for her to be able to go?" I asked.

"Once we get her dressed and in the wheelchair she can go. The wheelchair has to stay here though."

If he didn't stop with the corny shit, I was gonna put his ass in the hospital. I put the cup down and headed back out of the door to get the car.

"I'm going to get the truck now. See y'all downstairs. Did you want this drink now or do you want me to put it in the truck?"

"You can put it in the car."

I was happy as hell that we weren't gonna have to spend anymore nights in here. After getting the truck I pulled up to the front Adrian was coming out of the door with Grace's bag. The nurse was pushing her out in the wheelchair. I took the bag from Adrian putting it in the back seat of the truck. The nurse and I helped Grace get into the passenger's seat.

"I'll call you tomorrow. I'm sure you want to sleep in a regular bed without someone coming in poking on you every four hours. You need to rest and relax," Adrian told her as she stuck her head into the passenger's side window to give Grace a kiss on the cheek.

"Ok I love you friend," Grace said as she rolled the window up and I pulled off.

"Are you happy to get out of there?"

"Hell yes, I feel like I just broke out of jail."

"Do you need anything before I take you in?"

"No, I do want to thank you from the bottom of my heart for being by my side."

"I appreciate that you're thanking me but, you don't need to. You're not in this alone. That baby is half mine so I'm going to make sure this is as easy as it can be for you both. You will never have anything to worry about when it comes to you or my child."

"I know I can be difficult but, if you just be patient with me, I'm working on that part."

"Does that mean we're going steady and you're my girlfriend?" I asked laughing.

"You're crazy," she said laughing.

"I'm just saying. You're already pregnant so we're past the just talking phase. You're gonna be staying in the house with me until the baby comes so we may as well be going steady at least."

"Who says going steady? We can get to know each other better and all that while I'm in the house with you. I need to go to my place to get some of my things though. I don't know how I'm going to do that on bedrest," she sighed.

"Don't worry about none of that. I already had most of your clothes and shit moved into the house. Your car is in the garage. I didn't put a stop on your mail, but you can do that online. You might want to just have your mail sent to my house instead. All that is up to you."

"Wow thank you," she said.

"I told you already that you don't need to do that."

"Okay."

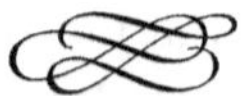

race

I couldn't believe all this shit that Gully had done while I was in the hospital. Walking into his house I thought he was exaggerating when he said he had some of my clothes and things brought to his house. Walking in the room that he had set up for me I could swear that all of my clothes were here. I don't know where he thought I was going with me being on bedrest.

"Germain how did you know what to bring?" I asked because I just had to know.

"I hit Adrian up and told her to grab you some clothes to bring here. I also made sure that she left all the thot shit right where it was. You're pregnant and there ain't shit sexy about a pregnant woman dressing like a damn thot."

He was shaking his head as he talked. I had no other choice but, to laugh at him. There was no way he could even think that I had some thot wear. I didn't tell him that though. It felt good seeing him riled up due to the thought of me wearing some small clothes. He said out of his mouth that we were just going steady, but he was acting like we were in a full-fledged relationship. It scared me a little bit thinking about being in a relationship. The last relationship didn't end well, and I wasn't trying to bring my issues from that relationship into a new one. This was something that was unexpected to me. I was fine with being alone for a while but, here comes Gully changing shit up.

"I appreciate that you care enough to even be upset but, I don't own any thot clothes."

I had to tell him because he was going to drive himself and me crazy.

"Come here let me talk to you. You need to understand that you being here and on bedrest means just that. I have you set up to where you have a video call meeting with your managers at the lounge on Tuesday and Thursday. That way you can prepare for the weekend and after the weekend to go over the numbers and whatever plans you want them to do. I'm not trying to run your life or nothing but, it's not all about you it's about the person that I want to see in some months from now. You're gonna be pissed with me more days than you're happy I'm sure. I have the doctor on speed dial, so I know what he needs for you to do and not to. I just need you to understand that. I have no issue with you coming out of the room but, ain't no outside going on. Your room has everything that you need I made sure of it. I also did the nursery for the baby. Do you want to go see it now?"

"Yeah, then I'm gonna take a shower and get myself together."

We walked to a room across from the room that he had me set up in. I wanted to ask why I was in another room but, I left it alone. I kept hearing Rick in my head telling me to let the man lead. I kept my mouth shut. It was hard as hell to do but, I did it.

The room was absolutely beautiful. Since I was only ten minutes pregnant the room was done in light shades of yellow, green, and off white. There were pampers with wings flying around some clouds. The furniture in the room was all white. He had a wall of pampers and baby wipes already. This room took so much thought to put together that it touched my heart. Before I knew it, my ass was standing in the room crying. I was happy but, the tears weren't about the happiness. It was about relief. Standing here I finally understood that I wasn't in this alone. It's one thing to hear that someone has your back because people say that all the time just like when they say call me if you need anything. Nine times out of ten they don't mean it. You could call and no one will answer the phone or if they answer they're telling you a ton of excuses as to why they can't help you. I was ready for the excuses and the broken promises. As I stood here it hit me that he meant every word that he said.

"Come on man. Don't tell me you're gonna be one of these pregnant chics that cry during the commercials and shit like that. I ain't gonna be able to deal with the tears and shit. You can curse me out and all that other shit. You can even get pissed and throw shit. It's the crying that I can't deal with," he told me with a pleading look on his face.

"I doubt I'll be crying the whole time. Right now, I'm just emotional. I'll be okay. I'm gonna go take a shower. The room is absolutely gorgeous," I told him.

"Let me know if you need some help," he told me as I walked away from him.

I walked in the room shaking my head. I couldn't do anything but, thank the lord that I never got pregnant by Blaine. If that had happened, I can almost guarantee that I would've gone to the abortion clinic. I had to make sure that I was going to continue to put my best foot forward during my time here.

OOOO

After taking a shower and getting in the bed that I was doomed to spend what seemed like the rest of my life in I went straight to sleep. Gully came in to bring me some food. He didn't wake me but, he left the food on the bedside table in a covered tray. I woke up sometime during the night to eat it. The first thing this morning Adrian was here to spend some time with me. I don't know if Gully was still here or not but, he never came in the room that day. I was happy to see Adrian.

"Are you still in the bed and following directions? Your hard-headed ass is probably in here trying to rearrange the closet and the furniture," Adrian joked.

She knew me so well because I was thinking about organizing the closet this morning after I ate the rest of my food. I laughed at her but, she knew she was right.

"Whatever heifer, you always trying to put the light on me. I know you're over there holding out on me."

"What are you talking about?"

"Russ," was all I said. Since she wanted to act like I had forgotten about the looks that were exchanged between them. She rolled her eyes and took a deep breath.

"Russell and I know each other from our past."

"Russell? Who the hell is Russell?" I asked laughing.

"You make me sick. Russell is his government name."

"Of course, continue though, what type of history do y'all have?"

I was wondering because I knew most of Adrian's history unless she had been keeping somethings from me. I was starting to feel like that's what this mess was with Adrian and Russell. It was something that she never told me about but, why? I knew about how her mom treated her. I also knew that the treatment caused her to go away to college as opposed to her staying home. We were both running from something out of high school. I was running from my family, which I thought was nosey, and overbearing at the time and she was running from her mom's bullshit.

"You thought that I left for college to get away from my mom but, she wasn't the only reason. I was also broken hearted after getting an abortion to get rid of the baby that Russell had put in me."

"WHAT THE FUCK DID YOU SAY?"

I didn't mean to yell at her. It surprised me hearing those words come from her mouth. *How the hell did she handle going through that alone? Was I that bad of a friend that she didn't want me to know? What was really going on?*

"Why are you yelling at me? Keep playing you're gonna make *Killmonger* bring his ass in here."

The next second after she said that the door flew open.

"Adrian, if you're gonna have her in here yelling and shit I'm gonna put your ass on the *'do not let in'* list. She can't be getting all excited and shit. You better not have her in here lusting after some naked niggas with they dicks out and shit either. If she yells again, I'm putting your ass out," he said before he slammed the door shut behind him when he left. Adrian and I looked at each other and fell out laughing.

"That nigga is crazy. I hope my god child doesn't come out all fucked up in the head because of him. Where the hell did the naked niggas comment come from? What are you in here doing Grace?" Adrian asked still laughing.

"We're not talking about him right now. What is the tea on you and Russ? Granted it's some old ass tea but, I still want to know."

Adrian rolled her eyes again then started to tell me about the history between her and Russell. She was emotional while telling me everything. The way she was talking I knew that the years that had passed meant nothing. She was hurting like this all went down last week. I held her hand the whole time.

"I don't know what to do at this point," she said wiping the tears from her cheeks. I held her in my arms. It hurt me that my friend was hurting so bad. I could understand her pain. I know that seeing him only brought everything back.

"Have you talked to him since the parking garage?"

"He's been sending me text messages. You know stuff like good morning, how was your day, and shit like that. Nothing major."

"You need to talk to him. I'm saying sit down and talk about everything you're feeling. Don't hold anything back. You've been carrying that burden for too long. You know now that he's aware what happened. You're not hurting alone in this."

"I just don't know how to put it in words when he's in front of me. This is the man that took my virginity. It's stupid that I still have feelings for him. I haven't seen or talked to him in god knows how long but I love him. I'm one of those stupid ass life-time chics."

"Wait a minute. Russ was at the grand opening with Gully. Where the hell were you? Why didn't y'all run into each other?" I asked.

I was confused as hell when I thought about it. I remember her being there. We talked in my office; we even went down to the floor together. I didn't remember her leaving well, telling me that she was leaving.

"I saw him. I didn't look to see who he was with. I just knew that I couldn't face him that night and mess up the opening. If we would've seen each other we were gonna fight because I would've slapped the shit out of him. I didn't anticipate on him coming to the hospital room. I wasn't prepared at all for that. I couldn't jump on him then either. Seeing him when I got out of the elevator, so close to him, made me freeze."

"Please tell me you're gonna talk to him," I told her.

"I will I promise," she said.

For all of our sakes I hope she did. The last thing I needed was the both of them getting here and causing a scene. Only time will tell though.

CHAPTER 17

drian

Sitting in my car in front of Gully's house. I didn't know why I was just sitting there but, I couldn't get myself to the point of leaving. I put my head against the steering wheel in an effort to get my nerves together. I wouldn't have felt this way if we didn't just discuss the situation with Russell. After all these years just talking about it was draining to me mentally and physically. There was a tapping on my window. I looked up at Russell standing outside of my car with his hands in the pockets of his jeans.

"Get out and come ride with me."

This nigga didn't give me a chance to respond to him. He just walked away. His arrogance got on my damn nerves but, I remember a time when it was the sexiest thing on him. I got out of the car and slow walked to his car. He was standing at the passenger side door with it open. I rolled my eyes at him and he was just smirking at me. He took hold of my arm before I got in the car. When I turned to face him, I was bracing for him to say something slick. Instead he kissed me. After separating from me he looked at me like he could fuck my soul out of me right in front of Gully's house. He licked his lips then smiled. He got in the car and pulled off.

"Where are you taking me?"

"You should've asked that before you got in the car. Don't worry about it I'm not gonna kill you or anything. Why did you get in the car with me in the first place?"

"You didn't give me an option."

"You always have an option. You could've pulled off on my ass instead of getting in here with me. I was expecting you to lay my ass out but, I'm loving just being around you lil baby," he said with a smile.

Hearing him call me lil baby was enough to make the tears come. I tried to quickly wipe them away but, when he took my hand in his and kissed the back of it, I realized I wasn't quick enough. Why was I sitting here with him? Why did I feel like I wanted to bare my soul to him?

"Did you ever get married? Do you have any kids?"

I only asked that because it was one of the first things that came to mind when I first saw him. The more I tried not to think about it the more I thought about it. It had become an endless battle.

"No."

"Why not?"

I could see how uncomfortable he was becoming. If he didn't want to talk then he could take me back to my car and life could go on. He adjusted in his seat, played with his right ear like he used to do when things got too deep for him.

"I didn't get married or have any kids because I didn't find anyone that did what you do for me."

"You don't have to bullshit me. When I left, I was just turning eighteen. You were the man to see in the hood. I'm sure there was some older female that could please you in all the ways a man needs to be pleased better than I ever could."

"There you go. It wasn't about your age, my age, or anybody else's age. I was in love with you before we did anything physical. You had my head gone and you didn't even know it. That day I went to your mom's house I was coming to get you. I was gonna take you to my place and keep you there. Those days that I wasn't able to talk to you had me feeling all types of fucked up. I came to get you because I couldn't take it anymore. When she told me that you left, I went back home and stayed for damn near three weeks. I wasn't thinking about how young you were and maybe I should've. I could only think about how my damn heart had just left me. You know that's what you are right, my heart? Nothing has changed that, and I doubt anything will."

Looking out of the window I thought about what my life could've been if I stayed here. Grace and I would've gone to Virginia State University. I would've still gotten my master's in education to be a high school guidance counselor. We had everything planned out. All that changed in a blink of an eye.

"I sat there for a day watching you call me. I wanted to pick up the phone and see what you had to say."

"Why didn't you? All of this could've been avoided."

"No, it couldn't. If we didn't break up, then it was only a matter of time before another female came long saying things about me that only you should know. We needed that time apart. I know I needed to grow and figure out who I was as a woman not the young girl that you claimed to be so in love with," I told him.

Everything I said is the truth. It took a lot of nights of tears and buckets of ice cream but, now I understood that all of this was part of god's plan.

"Nah, I don't believe that."

"Think about it Russell. If we would've stayed together how would I know that you couldn't live without me. How would you know that no woman does what I do for you? How would you know that I was the one that did all the right things for you? I was just getting out of high school. My entire life was in front of me. As much as I hate to admit it my mother was right. I needed that time on my own to get to know me on my own."

He listened to me but, I could tell he wasn't feeling what I was saying. It took me a while to even understand who I am as a woman. The pain that I felt behind Russell was all a part of my growing process. I understood that now. It all became clear to me one of those nights of me crying my eyes out. Caretha thought that she was ripping us a part when she was actually ensuring that once we did find each other again that we would be more solid than anyone ever thought we could be.

"I suppose that's one way of looking at it. I just need you to know that I'm gonna do everything in my power to keep you with me. If we have to go down to city hall and get married as soon as that motherfucker opens, then that's what we're gonna do. I hope you called all your niggas to let them know that I'm back."

"I don't have any niggas. You're the one with all the hoes. How's Caretha?"

"I don't know how her ass is doing. I haven't seen her since that day you told me about her coming to your mom's house. I still can't believe she did that shit. I never knew that she knew about you. Come to find out she went through my phone one time while I was sleeping. The fucked up thing about it is she was more upset about your age than anything else. I was never in a relationship with her but, for some reason you make her ass crazy. There have been times when we've seen each other and I was with other women but, she never said anything to me about it. When it comes to you, she just gets crazy. The only thing she kept repeating was that you were just a kid. It didn't matter what age you were. You always acted more adult than your age. Now you're talking bout how we needed that time apart. I just might have to thank her ass for doing the shit she did," he said with a smirk.

"You and her don't need to be around each other anymore. She served her purpose," I told him.

He laughed at me and shook his head. Watching him laugh made me realize that right here with him is where I belong. I've loved him since the first day we met. Just like he couldn't find a person to fill the void I left; I couldn't find anyone to live up to Russell. There was always something wrong with the men I came across. I even stopped talking to one guy because the cologne that Russell wore didn't smell the same on him. There was one guy who tried to call me lil' baby but, I shut that down because it didn't sound right coming from him.

"You don't have to be jealous of her or anyone else. In my eyes and soul, you're in a class of your own. You're above all of them."

"You don't have to gas me up. I know you love me just like I still love you. We can leave it at that. All that extra shit is unnecessary."

"Unnecessary? Nah, it definitely ain't that, you need to know what it really is when it comes to you. I still rode past your mom's every now and then to see if I could run into you. I would be on date or knee deep in some pussy and still think about you. You were the only one that knew everything about me. You knew about all the chicks I was fucking with back then. Just like you knew that I stopped fucking with them when you gave me yourself. You gave me the most precious gift that I could ever ask for."

We sat there looking at each other. I didn't realize that he had stopped driving until he took the keys out of the ignition. I looked around not recognizing where we were. We were parked in a driveway of a two-story house. The yard was the perfect shade of green. It was trimmed perfectly, with various shades of roses to add to the curb appeal. The bricks of the home were beige in color which matched perfectly with the gray shutters. I would never think to put gray shutters on a house but, it looked good.

"Whose house is this? Who lives here?" I asked. He didn't answer but, he got out of the car opening my door for me to get out. I know he heard me the first time, so I wasn't going to repeat my questions. I watched as he put the key in the door. Walking into the house the place was spotless. There wasn't much furniture in it at all. It didn't look lived in. "Russell whose house is this?" I asked.

"Yours and it's paid for. I bought this house the day before I came to your moms to get you. I had to show you that I was dead ass about you and I being together. I was going to ask you to marry me and everything. I kept the place hoping that you would come back to me. It's not decorated because you should be the one to make this place a home."

He put a set of keys in my hand.

"It can't be a home if you're not living here with me," I said with a smile.

"Are you asking me to shack up with you?"

"No, I'm asking you to help me make this house a home Russell. I can't stay here alone there's too much space."

He picked me up and spun me around then let me down to kiss me deeply. I was finally going to get my happily ever after.

ully

Grace and I were getting closer than I ever thought was possible. We would sit up at night looking at movies and eating popcorn. The shit was corny as hell when I thought about it but, when the shit was going down it just felt right. She had been in my room for the past three days. I didn't want her to go back to her room. I knew that with Grace that was always going to be a possibility. I could see that she was making an effort to put the best that she had to share with me into this relationship. I had been here with her for the most part. I would leave to go get something to eat or stop by the office but, that was about it. Usually I would get tired of a chic constantly being in my space but, with Grace I was dreading her moving back to her place. I could hear Grace on her phone asking who was calling and not saying anything. There was someone calling her off and on lately. They would only breathe or just sit on the phone and let the TV in the background play loud. She didn't think I knew because I was still waiting on her to tell me about it.

"When were you gonna tell me about the phone calls?" I asked her.

"I was gonna tell you but, I don't have anything to tell. I don't know who it is or why anyone would want to prank call me. I don't have any issues with anyone. It doesn't make sense."

"I'm listening to you but, when people have issues with you, they don't always tell you about them. Shit, they may not like you because your name starts with a G. I've been waiting on you to say something. You need to get your number changed," I told her.

"If I get my number changed that means I'm gonna have to get it to all my business contacts, distributors, employees, family, and all that is too much of a hassle."

"Nah, if they want to continue to do business with you, they can get the new number. You sound crazy talking about it's too much of a hassle. It'll be a damn hassle if you get hurt or stalked because you don't want to change your number. If my child gets hurt because you don't want to do what's best for y'all then we are gonna have a big ass problem. Do you want problems with motherfuckers that don't give a shit about you or me? Which one is it?"

She shook her head and took a breath. She could act like I wasn't acting in her best interest all she wants to. Grace had to stop thinking that it was only her now because it's not. My child's life is at stake here.

"I can change it."

"You don't have a clue who it could be calling you? Have you talked to Urkel from the hospital? Do you think it could be him?" I was trying not to go off the deep end but, this shit was fucking with me.

"I haven't talked to him at all. I still don't understand why he was at the hospital in the first place. He wasn't that caring or even to the point where he showed he cared when we were together."

"What happened with y'all?"

"Our relationship was built on a lie. Well, I saw it as a lie. His parents found out that my dad was the District Attorney. They found this out before he and I started dating. His parents are rich and all about image. They only wanted their son with someone who would help elevate his image as well as theirs. I met them at a basketball game one night. I spoke to Blaine because we had a few classes together. We talked for a few minutes and then I went on about my way. A few weeks later he started hitting on me and stuff. It took a while, but we started going out. The more we hung out with each other the more I realized that he wasn't who he portrayed himself to be. He wanted to showboat for the people around him all the time. I was more of a trophy piece than anything. He would constantly 'remind' me about his accomplishments and stuff. It was like we couldn't go anywhere without him bragging about himself.

"I already wasn't too thrilled about being with him then when we had sex something was off. I couldn't figure out if it was the lack of passion, coordination, or just him. We had sex a few more times before I just started not having sex with him at all. He never bothered me about it though. Adrian would always joke that he was gay and in the back of the closet because of his family. Come to find out he's really gay. I haven't told anyone but you though. I couldn't tell Adrian because she wouldn't hesitate on letting him know that she knows his secret. He said something to me about me coming to dinner with him and his family but, I avoided answering him. I know the only reason he wants me to go is because he still hasn't told his family that we broke up or that he's gay or bisexual," she told me.

I wasn't expecting her to say that his ass was gay for real. He did seem little on the sensitive side but, hey you never know these days.

"Why do you say that he wouldn't be the one calling? Never put anything past anyone. You never know what a person will do when their back is against the wall. Have you gone out with him since y'all broke up? What reason does he have to ask you to put on a show now for?" I asked.

"He isn't built like that," she said as she shrugged her shoulders.

I knew she was telling me the truth but, I also saw there were holes in the story. There had to be a reason why he came to her and no one else. Don't most gay guys have a female best friend? Why couldn't he ask another friend or whatever? Something wasn't adding up. Grace was so sure that it wasn't him, but I was almost certain that it was him or somebody he knew. Grace's circle was tight so it couldn't be no jealousy shit going on with the folks around her. He had to have something to do with the phone calls but, why now? The doorbell chimed letting me know that Adrian and Russ were here. The ladies were going to stay here while Russ and I went out to check out a jobsite. The foreman had called to say he needed to talk to both of us. I opened the door to see them kissing.

"Yo, stop doing that shit on my porch," I said to them.

"Where's my best friend?" Adrian asked walking past me.

"Come on man, I left the gate open. We ain't got time for you to get a quickie in," Russ said joking as always.

"I'm coming. You look like you were about to have a quickie on my porch."

"Nah, we not on that yet, we're just trying to get past some shit," he said low enough for Adrian not to hear him.

I nodded my head and went to grab my things. I gave Grace a kiss on the cheek and we were on our way. I was sure to close the gate after we pulled out.

"Are you gonna tell me the deal with you and Adrian? You've been real hush about it. I think you and her dry humping on my porch means I need some things explained."

"Dry humping? Nigga, we were just kissing stop being dramatic. Nah, Adrian is my lil baby she always has been. We started messing around when she was in high school. Her mom didn't like the age difference but, she got more pleasure from giving us hell about it. She never called the cops on my ass. Then I go to her house one day and her mom tells me she left town. It fucked me up because she had just told me she was pregnant and shit. Seeing her in the hospital was the first time I saw her since she told me that shit. We talked and come to find out Caretha's scandalous ass went to Adrian's mom's house telling her a bunch of bullshit. Adrian got an abortion and left town without even talking to my ass."

"Damn, that's some shit for your ass. I know you fucked Caretha up. I told you her ass wasn't right a long time ago."

"Yeah, I went to see her ass," he said glancing over at me as he drove.

"I hope y'all get it right this time. What the hell do Chuck need to see both of us for?" I asked.

Chuck was the foreman of the jobsite that we were headed to. We've been working with him since we started this business. Chuck was about his work and wasn't going to tolerate bullshitting from his crew. He was old enough to retire but, he worked like he was still trying to impress us. He had the respect and confidence of Russ and me. When he called, I know it had to be something major for him to call to see both of us.

"I don't know I was about to ask you the same thing. I guess we'll find out when we get up here. The shit is coming along well. With the building being by the water and shit means we're gonna make a killing and gain that recognition that we fucking deserve. Once they see how we made it all come together nobody can sleep on us out here."

Russ was right this shit was gonna put our company on the map like a motherfucker.

"Do you miss it sometimes?"

"Miss what? I know you're not talking about the streets. Nah, I don't miss that shit. I've gotten used to pulling up next to a cop car at a red light and straight throwing that bitch a head nod. I remember times when we would see a cop car and go the long way just so we don't past them. Especially with Adrian coming back into my life I damn sure don't want to be out there. What about you?"

"Hell nah, I got a kid on the way and they don't need to know about that part of my life. I'm gonna leave my kids a legal empire that's what I'm gonna do," I told him.

"Yeah that's what's up. Let's go see what the hell is going on," Russ said as he parked.

uss

The building was coming together. The more I saw it get closer to completion the more I wanted to get a condo in the building. It was on the water so the views from most of the condos would be spectacular. Every condo had a balcony even the smaller ones. The place was going to make a killing.

"Hey gentlemen, I didn't think you would come until tomorrow," Chuck said as he shook our hands.

"No need to put off for tomorrow what you can do today. There's no time like the present. What's going on? You have both of us wondering what made you call," Gully said.

"There's been a guy coming up here. He's not the investor because I know him and he's not gonna get out of the car to get any mud on his expensive ass shoes. When I asked the guy who he was and what business did he have up here he said that he was up here with y'all's permission. The first time I planned on calling you both to ask about it but, I got to working and forgot all about it. When he came up here today, I ran his ass out of here. I called because y'all need to know what's going on. He didn't touch any of the equipment or blueprints because I was stuck to his ass like glue the whole time he was here. People claim that the music business is the shadiest business but, real estate isn't a piece of peach pie. I've seen some slick stuff go on in all these years. You two need to be on your shit with this project."

"Do you have a picture of the guy?" I asked.

"Yeah, it's in my phone. Let me go get it."

He walked away and Gully and I were both in our own thoughts trying to figure out what the hell is going on. My phone started going off showing me that Adrian was trying to FaceTime me.

"Hey baby," I answered.

Instead of looking at her face I was looking at the ceiling. I could hear a lot of screaming. Gully rushed over to me looking over my shoulder.

"Grace what the hell is going on over there," Gully asked.

"You stupid bitch. How could you get pregnant by some thug ass nigga? You're a tainted woman now. Just another piece of ghetto trash. You ruined everything," we heard a male voice say.

We were both in the car speeding to the house. This shit was definitely going to pull the old us out. A person fucking with the woman you love will bring the worst traits out of any nigga. I could see Gully tapping away at his phone. Weaving in and out of traffic we got to the house in no time. The first thing we noticed was that the gate was still closed. I know that the gate was closed after we left. If it was closed now and then that means someone had to slip through the gate while Gully was putting his clothes on. There's no other explanation for it. I left the car running and barely put it in park before Gully and I were out of it. We ran up in the house looking for the girls. Hopefully the nigga was still in the house. I don't think they knew that Adrian had dialed my number. I wanted to yell out to them to see where they were but, if I did that then that would give the intruder a heads up that we were here. We inched our way upstairs pausing when we heard voices. They were faint but we still heard them. Once we made it to the master bedroom I threw up at the site before me.

Adrian was in the corner with bruises all over her face, the shirt she had on was ripped and revealed the scratches on her chest. Her eyes were closed my heart left my body as I looked at her. She looked like she was dead already. I forced my legs to move and the first thing I did when I got to her was checked to see if she was breathing. Indeed, she was still alive.

"Baby, you gotta get up. What the fuck happened? Who did this shit? All this fucking blood everywhere," I heard Gully say. I looked up to see what he was talking about and Grace was covered in blood from her stomach down. She was also unconscious. The way Gully was losing his shit she had to be unconscious to continue to lay still like she was. I called for an ambulance to come. I knew that the police would most likely show up as well. I didn't like dealing with them but, right now I'm praying extra hard for them to get here. Gully was holding on to Grace rocking her back and forth. He was now covered in her blood but, he wasn't going to let her go. I could see the tears rolling down his face. I scooped up Adrian in my arms took her to the bathroom in the room and put her in it. I turned the water on after making sure her face was under the faucet. Three seconds after turning the water on she started swinging wildly and shit like she was drowning. I had to fight her off just to turn the water off.

"What the fuck? Are you trying to kill me?" She asked as she was trying to catch her breath.

"Nah, I was just trying to wake you up."

"Oh shit," she said. She hopped up and tried to make her way to the room where Grace and Gully were. She took one step and fell to the floor.

"What's the matter?"

"My foot, I can't put any pressure on my foot. Where's Grace is she okay?" She asked. She was beginning to panic as she asked constantly was Grace okay. I picked her up taking her back into the bedroom so she could see Grace. I didn't want her to look at her that way but, she was there when the shit happened. She was going to be worried until she laid eyes on her. When she saw all the blood and shit, she broke down. "I should've done more. Why didn't I fight harder? Oh God please don't take my sister/friend away from me," she sobbed. I sat down in the chair in the corner of the room. She had her hands wrapped so tight around my neck that I knew she wasn't going to let me go. The paramedics and police finally arrived. One went to Grace while the other came over to where I was with Adrian.

"Ma'am can you tell me where you're hurting?" He asked her.

"It's just my foot. You need to be over there helping my friend. I'll be fine he can carry me to the ambulance or wherever. She needs help. She can't lose the baby!" She screamed.

The poor paramedic was so thrown off by Adrian's words and tears that he started stuttering. It had to be his first week or something.

"Just go over there I'll carry her to the ambulance. Better yet, just tell me what hospital y'all are going to and we'll be there."

"No, we need to follow them," Adrian cut in.

"We'll be in my car waiting to follow y'all," I told him. He nodded his head. I picked up Adrian and took her to the car. She was worried to pieces about Grace and the baby. I wasn't a rocket scientist but, it didn't look like they were going to be able to save the baby. This was going to crush her and Gully. I was gonna be right there bringing pain to whoever did this shit.

"It's my fault. I should've brought my gun with me. I left it home because I thought nothing could happen to us here. That was so stupid of me. When I leave the hospital, I'm gonna track his ass down and gut him like a damn fish. That nigga has something worse than death coming to him."

"You know who it was that came in the house?"

"Yeah, it was Blaine's punk ass and another guy. I couldn't figure out who the other guy was but, it was Blaine for sure. I don't understand how he could go through all of this just because he didn't want his parents to know that he was gay. If you ask me, they already know and he's just being the punk that he is by not telling them."

"What all was he saying? I could make out some stuff but, I don't know the full story," I said to Adrian once we got in the car to wait for the paramedics to come out with Grace.

"We were watching TV and we heard a door close. I had a bat and Grace had a knife. Even though she was on bed rest she wasn't gonna let me go check out the noise on my own. The lights were off because we were in the room. I was coming around the corner and someone snatched the bat out of my hands. It happened so fast that all I could do was yell for Grace to get back in the room. I started fighting the one guy. When I knocked him out with a jar of mayonnaise; I ran to the room that Grace was in. I could see him sitting on top of her hitting her over and over. I jumped on his back and started clawing at his eyes. I was hitting him everywhere I could think of just trying to get him off of Grace. Then something hit me in the head. I fell over and started kicking at anything moving. It was working until Blaine hit me with the bat. That's what knocked me out. I should've done more to help Grace. Now she's gonna lose the baby and it's all my fault," Adrian broke down onto my shoulder.

None of this was anyone's fault but this nigga Blaine and whoever was with him. That's some bogus ass shit to do just because someone doesn't want you anymore. That shit was a violation to every man code there was. Oh, hell yeah, this nigga was gonna feel my pain.

"You can follow us. Try to keep up, turn your hazard lights on," one of the paramedics said. I gave him a head nod and pulled out behind them.

ully

This shit can't be happening right now. I was having and out of body experience. I knew I was sitting in the back of the ambulance holding Grace's hand. I knew that she had lost the baby by all the blood that she had lost. I just needed her to come out of this alive. We could always make another baby. It was Grace that was irreplaceable in my world. Grace was the one that left me terrified when I saw her on the bed covered in blood. I should've known that the man above had some turmoil for my ass to go through before I got to my happy hood ending. It was too peaceful for Grace and me to get to the love and happiness just by her being in my house on bedrest. It was too simple to be in the plans for my life. Looking down at her laid out on the stretcher I knew that she was going to be okay. I already had come to accept that the baby wasn't going to make it. I was a hood nigga that didn't do the optimistic side of life often. This was a time that I knew without a doubt that there was no way the baby at this early in the pregnancy could survive.

"Grace we're gonna get through this. Do you hear me baby mama? You will always be my baby mama. You don't have shit to worry about in life ever if I have any say so. Just make sure you come back to me," I whispered in her ear then kissed her on her lips.

The ambulance stopped and the doors flew open. The hospital staff and the paramedics pulled the stretcher that carried the unconscious love of my life off. They rushed her into the hospital doors. My heart and head were telling me that I should run in there behind them but, my feet weren't co-operating. Instead of walking into the hospital I dropped to my knees and prayed. I haven't prayed since I was being forced to go to church with my grandparents. I could hear my grandmother telling me 'when you don't know what else to do it's time to pray'. Losing a child and possibly the woman I love left me at loss trying to decide what to do. I wasn't a doctor so I couldn't help them save her but, I knew the lord could help. Granted I haven't seen the inside of church or chapel unless it was for a funeral but, I know the man above still knew who I was.

"Lord I come to you the only way I know how. I'm in a parking lot of a hospital on my knees. I don't care about the people looking at me like I'm some crackhead or homeless person. All I care about is if you bring Grace back to me. I know you made her for me. She may be mean, sassy with her words, and sexy with everything she puts on but, I know you made her just for me. I'm the only one that can handle her. You didn't put her in my world just to take her away so quickly. I need to show her that love is right here for her. She's too scared to love me and I know that. I'm not going anywhere she's gonna see it but, I need her alive and down here with me to show her," I prayed.

I stood up to see Russ standing there looking heavy in the face.

"It's gonna be okay Grace and the baby will be fine," he said trying to comfort me.

"Nah, man I could feel that the baby was gone when I walked in the house. It's Grace I'm worried about. I talked to her the whole time I was with her. I know she heard me I just need her to come back to me. Nothing else matters right now. Did Adrian say who it was? I think I have an idea but, I just need to know if they knew them."

"Adrian said one of them was some cat named Blaine she didn't know who the other one was though."

Hearing the name Blaine made me want to kill that Urkel looking motherfucker with my own hands. Thinking about what Grace told me about him I knew he wasn't going to go far. His punk ass couldn't even cut the strings from his parents to tell them he was gay. He was one of those needy rich kids that wouldn't dare leave his family. I knew he was too fucking cocky to think that he would get caught. That just means that I had time to find out what's going on with Grace before I went to kill the nigga. I had to make sure I had eyes on him though. I sent a few text messages out to some guys that I trusted that would keep me posted on this nigga's movements. I needed to have confidence that they weren't gonna be somewhere fucking off while on assignment. Once I got the text confirming they were on it I was ready to go into the hospital. I wasn't really ready but, I had to suck up my feelings and get my ass in there. Walking in I could see that Grace's family hadn't started showing up yet. I'm sure that Adrian called at least one of them. They were sure to come in with their questions. I didn't have answers, not yet.

Taking a seat in the waiting area there was a white couple in there but other than that it was empty. I didn't know who they were waiting on but, they had no idea of the shit they were about to witness. I know if one of Grace's family members come at me sideways, I was gonna mop this room with their asses. The only one that could get a pass was Auntie GiGi other than that they all could get it. I needed to blow off some anger, so it wasn't gonna take much. I started rubbing my temples to fight off the headache that was approaching the door flew open. *Let the bullshit begin!*

"You said you would protect her with your life. Tell me why she's in there fighting for her life and you're sitting here unhurt and looking unfazed like a motherfucker?" One of her cousins said busting up in here like he mattered. I continued to rub my temples ignoring his ass.

"Ali sit your ass down somewhere. Grace is back there fighting for her life. Do you think this man let whatever happen to her just happen while he watched? I told you not to come in here with that shit. We need to find out what the fuck happened. Accusing him is not a good way to start. Now sit your wanna be thug ass down. I might just let him kick your ass because that last ass kicking you got must've wore off," the older guy said. I knew he was an uncle because he favored the rest of the family. I just hadn't met him yet. He watched the guy sit down then he turned to me. I stood up because he needed to be shown respect and I wasn't gonna let no man look down on me. He held his hand out for me to shake with a smirk on his face. "How are you holding up? I'm Grace's Uncle Gary. You must be the man that my sister can't stop talking about," he said as we shook hands.

"I'm Germain but, everyone calls me Gully."

"Once everything settles down, we need to sit down and talk. That one over there is my punk ass son. Don't let his gorilla like build fool you. He's big for no damn reason. He's been getting his ass kicked for years. I've tried to show his ass how to fight but, all he wants to do is shoot. I keep telling him he needs to know what to do when he can't get to the gun. Hard-headed ass nigga, he gets that shit from his mama side. She's probably somewhere getting her ass kicked right now. I never hit the woman but, that was too much like right. Left me and went right into the fist of the nigga she's with now. She walking around telling everybody she's happy with black eyes and shit. I just don't understand it," he said shaking his head.

I didn't know if I was supposed to respond or just let his ass keep rambling. I looked at his son and shook my head. It's a damn shame that his own father was pulling his hoe card in public. I guess everything he was saying was true because the son didn't try to defend himself. Uncle Gary was right though because the nigga had to be all of six five and damn near three hundred pounds. He looked like he needed to be on someone's football team.

"Gary what did they say?" Auntie GiGi came in asking questions.

"I just got here. I had to stop him from fucking up your nephew," Uncle Gary told her. Auntie GiGi rolled her eyes and shook her head.

"I keep telling you that you and your brother are always claiming other people's kids. Ain't no way him or his hoe ass sister are any kin to us. You're not gonna get me started but ain't no hoe or punk in any of us. I'm tired of always having to explain that shit to y'all. He ain't my damn nephew just because you used to stick your small hot dog in his mama. I know those scamming bitches saw y'all coming a mile away. How the fuck you have all these kids and not one of them look like you or anyone in our family? They don't have y'all attitudes or nothing. You still claiming them though. I'm not doing that shit, talking about my nephew, negro please," Auntie GiGi said crossing her arms.

"Hey Auntie GiGi," I said trying to distract her from going in on her brother anymore.

"Hey baby, did that big, ugly, grown ass orphan say something to you? I ain't gonna fight no man but, I'll slap the shit out of his mama. Shit, it's her damn fault he alive right now. She should've told him who his real daddy is."

"Georgette!" Uncle Gary said.

"Gary! I know your name just like you know mine. I know who name you don't know though. The name of them kids' real daddy."

"I'm gonna kick your ass one of these days. Your mouth is terrible," Uncle Gary said.

"So is that permanent limp that you're gonna have once I shoot your ass if you ever lay a hand on me. I'm not gonna fight a man but, I'll shoot a nigga all day long if I have to. Go over there and sit with the big nigga in the corner that you've been sponsoring all his life."

Auntie GiGi was a complete mess out here. Uncle Gary shook his head at her.

"Keep it up and watch what happens."

"I'll start being scared tomorrow. I need to find out about my niece tonight," she said to him then turned to me. "Did the doctors say anything?"

"No but, I know that she's lost the baby. I knew it when I walked in that house. It's so fucked up. I was only gone for about thirty minutes when Russ got the call. If it wasn't something important, I wouldn't have left her," I explained.

I was having a hard time keeping my feelings in check. I knew no one here would look at me differently but, I had to be strong for Grace. She was gonna need me to be her backbone. I took a seat in the corner to myself. Gradually the rest of the family started filtering into the waiting area. I don't know how long it was before the doctor came in but, when he did, I was on my feet and in his face in a matter of seconds.

"What's going on with my niece?" Auntie GiGi asked the doctor.

"She's alive and stable. We couldn't save the fetus unfortunately. She lost a lot of blood. Whoever did this to her was trying to kill more than the baby. She doesn't have any broken bones but, she's gonna feel like it for at least a week. Her body needs rest. I elected not to put her in a medically induced coma yet. We will see how she does through the night before we decide on that permanently. Whoever Germain is she's been saying your name repeatedly. I suggest you go in there first once we get her settled. If you have any other questions just have one of the nurses call me. Actually, if you could follow me, I think her seeing you will help her relax more," he told me.

"I'm right behind you."

"Now before we go in here, I'm gonna let you know that she has bruises all over her body including her face. Because of the miscarriage we had to administer a D&C on her. I already informed her that there may or may not be some bleeding. It depends on the woman's body. Some women bleed heavy for a various amount of time. It can last for only a day or two or it can last for week. There are also others may bleed light or not at all. We cleaned her up of all the blood that was on her when she came in. I also had to put some stitches in her lip, but she still manages to say your name clear as day," he said as he opened the door to the room.

My blood pressure shot up thru the roof when I saw what her face looked like. I walked over to her bedside. Taking her hand in mine was a task because I didn't want to hurt her any more than she was already hurt.

"I'm sor…sorry," she moaned out.

"None of this is on you. You have nothing to be sorry for baby mama. I'm sorry for not protecting you like I should've," I told her.

"It was Blaine."

"I know Russ told me. You just worry about getting better I'll handle him," I told her.

She tried to smile at me. It was hard to sit here and look at her like this. At the same time there was no other place I wanted to be. I laid my head on her stomach until I dosed off with her rubbing my head with her good hand.

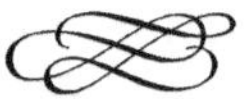

CHAPTER 21

*B*laine

I sat in the living room of my apartment. The lights were off, and I was just sitting here scared out of my mind. The flash backs of what I did haunted me. I should've listened to Max when he told me to just leave Grace alone. 'You can't make someone do anything they don't want to do' is what he told me. I didn't like when he got in his 'preachy' moods. I let what he said go in one ear and out of the other. Max didn't understand what it was like to live three different lives every day. I had my life with him which basically was only able to exist in our apartment or at his family's house. Then I had my other two lives which consists of my life around my family, the aspiring He would always tell me that he knew what it was like, but he didn't know shit. His folks were fine with him being gay and married to me. They came to the wedding, even gave us a big reception. He didn't have to deal with being born into a family of judgmental, prejudice strangers.

My parents would never be as welcoming as Max's. They wouldn't want to have him over for dinner or family game night. I know for a fact they would disown me without question. They are the reason I'm walking around everyday stressed in ways I never thought of. As if being a successful stockbroker isn't stressful enough. I had a mother who wanted grandkids, so she was sure to remind my sister and I of that daily. My father wanted me to play golf and drink beer with him and his buddies. Golf wasn't my thing it was just too damn hot most of the time. Beer is disgusting I would rather drink a mimosa or a martini. The third life was that of the faithful boyfriend to Grace. I had fucked that up years ago but, I was sure to keep in contact with her. Once she got over the hurt of finding out about Max we stayed in contact. She understood how much pressure my parents put on me, so she agreed to come to family functions with me. Grace had been telling me that I need to tell my parents. She would always say when she got in a new relationship our agreement would end. I just never thought she would actually get in another relationship.

Grace was a bit much to handle as far as being in a relationship. She was gorgeous there was no doubt about that. It was the part of her that was so driven and focused on the goals that she had set that caused the problem. She would rather create a business plan, look for a site for a new business to go or even invest in some stocks before she wanted to cuddle or even have sex. If I wasn't gay while we were together, we wouldn't have lasted as long as we did. She wasn't the type to make a man feel wanted or needed. I would tell her that all the time, but she was too stubborn to listen.

Max would listen to me complain, rant, and vent. There wasn't much else that he could do. I was a stockbroker but, the lifestyle that I lived was way over my pay grade. I'm not a regular working guy so for me not to have access to money would definitely be a major blow for me. Being born rich was more of a handicap for me than a blessing. My sister was the same way. She was living a life that wasn't what she chose either. My parents were going around town acting like they were so perfect when their children were fucked up mentally with no therapist in sight.

"Why are you in here in the dark?" Max asked me. I didn't

look his way or respond. He sat beside me taking my hand into his. "Baby what's wrong? You're scaring me," he said.

I looked at his pale skin, gray hair, and blue eyes and the caring that was permeating from him only broke my heart. Yes, my Max was a white man. Not only am I disgracing my family by being gay but being married to a white man is going to be seen as equally bad. There was no other way for me to tell him about what I did. I just had to push the words from my throat where they were currently stuck forming a knot.

"I went to Gully's place to confront Grace," I told him.

"I can look at you and tell that more happened than that. What else did you do?" He asked. A single tear from my right eye.

"I messed up everything. I messed it all up but, I didn't mean to."

"That's not telling me anything," he said.

"We stood outside for a while then we saw a car go through the gate. We were expecting the gate to close back but, it didn't. We were able to sip in before they came outside. After the car left, we got in through the back door. She was smiling and laughing talking about the baby she was carrying. She looked so damn happy. I've never seen her so happy before. Then she saw me. She looked scared at first but, I tried to calm her down telling her I was only there to talk. Things got out of hand when her friend started going off. Things got heated which lead to more arguing out of nowhere Tick slapped her friend. That's when everything completely went to shit. By the time I stopped myself Grace was covered in blood, Tick had been stabbed with a damn fork. The one thing we didn't count on was the gate being locked which meant we were trapped in there. When the car came back, we were able to slip out. We didn't wear masks or anything so it only a matter of time before he comes for me. I'm so sorry I should've listened to you," I told him.

"I told you to leave it alone. I remember telling you that

multiple times. On top of you doing that stupid shit you went and got your old fuck buddy to help you. How could you? The more I try to lead you in the right direction the more you go astray. You were not supposed to do anything to Grace. Her boyfriend isn't just some thug he's the thug that isn't a thug anymore. Him not being a thug anymore means nothing because all you have to do is mention his name and people get shook. You just messed up everything. Where was your sister when you were doing all of this?"

"She doesn't know anything."

"Not only did you put you and your fuck buddy's life in danger. You put hers in danger too. He's gonna know for sure that y'all are siblings now. I can bet you all the money I will ever have in life that he's gonna come for you. When he finds out who you are to Martina, he's gonna come for her ass too."

He was red in the face, it looked like he was debating on if he was going to try to beat my ass. I've never seen him so mad. He was walking around the house gathering up things and pulling out luggage.

"What are you doing?"

"I'm getting the fuck out of town. It was bad enough I helped you and your sister bury her old ass husband. That wasn't enough for you though you had to go mess with Grace. I'm not tarnishing my career for you or your stupid sister. I hope you come from under the hold that your parents have on you. It's just too bad that I'm not gonna be here to see it. If you had any sense you would find somewhere to go. Preferably, I need it to be in the opposite direction of me," he said packing up his stuff.

"Wait a minute you're my husband and we took vows for better or worse. We're in this together until death!"

I didn't mean to get loud but, it was pissing me off how he was ready to jump ship so easily.

"Oh you'll be dead in a week maybe two weeks tops. You think I'm gonna sit here and die with you. Oh no honey you got me messed up to the fullest. Me and my lily white ass is out of here. If you're still alive next month, I'll send the divorce papers for you to sign. I love you but I love living more," he said giving me a kiss.

I stood there in shock as the man I loved enough to marry walked out of my life.

CHAPTER 22

Martina

I paced the floor trying to think of a way I could get Gully to help me purchase this land. I even tried to think of a way we could move Lester's body before someone found it. If I would've known it would cause this much trouble, I would've buried his ass in the back yard. When I agreed to marry Lester, he wasn't supposed to live beyond three years. Come to find out him and my father concocted the whole story of him being ill with some type of cancer. The way they explained it to me was that since my parents were on their way to poor house Lester would pay my father to marry me. Being that he was dying anyway I wouldn't have to be married long. That's why I was messing around with Germain every chance I got. He used to always ask me what about my husband. If I even tried to do the tricks that I did on Germain in the bedroom to Lester, he would have a damn heart attack and die was the way I was thinking. That wasn't going to happen so I added something special to his food every chance I could. It took a little while but it worked.

Lester didn't have any living relatives well, besides me. If he would've died all of his money would've been allocated to the state. He didn't want that so he made out a will for everything to go to me and my father after we got married. I never understood why he and daddy were so close but, whatever. The night he finally died I was so nervous and scared that I called my brother to come help me do something with his body. The van that Lester had for no damn reason came in handy. It was parked in the garage, so we didn't have to try to conceal the body to get it in the van. We drove out to this remote undeveloped place not far from the city and buried his ass. Two days later I filed a missing persons report. I didn't find out until I filed the report that it takes ten years for someone that's missing to be declared legally dead and another ten before they can be presumed dead. I admit it was hasty of me to want to bury him with him being old as hell. If I would've thought things through, I would've just called the police and told them some believable story about how he died.

I fired his staff because I knew if he didn't come home soon, they would be asking questions. It's been ten months that he's been buried there and now the city wants to look into developing the land. Max was good for something because he worked for the city that's how I got the heads up that they were looking to develop the land. He told me that the best way to get rid of Lester's body was to buy the land, move the body, then sell it for a profit when the city starts trying to develop it. I had no clue how to go about buying or selling land so I was hesitant at first. Imagine my surprise when I finally started looking into buying the land it had already been sold with a new development being built on it as we speak. Of course the sarcastic humor of the Lord and all his angels wouldn't be what it was if any one other than Germain's company were the one's building on top of Lester's ass.

I know he thought that I wanted to get back with him but, that ain't what I wanted. Germain could get me in the bed any day of the week but, I'm not the relationship type of woman. I want to come and go as I please without anyone trying to figure out where I am.

Every time I went to see him, he was ducking and dodging me

like I wanted his dick again. If he was offering, I was surely going to take it but, that wasn't why I was reaching out to him. I just had to get him to understand that. Max told me that the city was going to start making offers to landowners early next year so that would be time enough for me to appear to be just another landowner. If that wasn't enough for me to worry about Germain has gone and got himself involved with the same girl that my brother had been parading around my parents as his girlfriend. I don't know why Blaine thought he was fooling somebody. I knew he was gay when he was in high school. I'm sure my parents know too but, they aren't gonna say anything if he doesn't. I would roll my eyes when our parents would ask him about Grace. He would always say some type of lie about why she wasn't around. My mother used to work in the law firm that Grace's father worked at before he was appointed the district attorney. I think my mother had a crush on Grace's dad but, who am I to call her out on her shit. When mom found out that Grace and Blaine were going to the same school, she was always saying how Grace would be the perfect match for him. Blaine being the mama's boy that he is made it his business to get in a glass with Grace. When she finally agreed to go out with him, he thought that was going to get my parents off his back. It only got worse because they started hounding him about grandkids. The doorbell chiming took me away from my pacing and thoughts. When I opened the door to see Blaine looking worried, I knew I had to brace myself for whatever he had to say.

"What happened?" I asked.

"I fucked up bad and now I might die," he said shocking me.

"I'm sure mommy and daddy aren't going to kill you because you're gay and married. They will disown you but, that may not last forever," I told him brushing him off. He was always getting dramatic about shit.

"No this isn't about that. I beat up Grace so bad I'm sure she lost the baby she was carrying. I didn't mean to everything happened so fast and I couldn't stop myself. I don't even remember half of it," he said.

"Grace who? I hope you're not talking about the same Grace that I think you're talking about," I told him. He nodded his head up and down.

"Blaine mommy and daddy finding out about you is the least of your worries. Germain is going to kill you I can promise you that," I told him.

"If he comes for me then he's coming for you too. He might not know we're brother and sister but, he's damn sure gonna find out. Once he does, he's gonna think that you tried to play him. So, if I'm gonna die, I'm not gonna do the shit alone Martina."

I was speechless because he was right and everything that we both were trying to hide was gonna come back on our asses.

"You have to leave just in case he's following you. We can't be seen together."

"What am I supposed to do if he's at my place when I get there?" He asked me.

"How the hell am I supposed to know? I guess you need to fight for your life. Just make sure you do it away from here," I told him.

He looked like he wanted to say something to me but he didn't. When he left my house I began wondering how the hell I was gonna get out of this.

race

I opened my eyes and the first thing I felt was Gully's head on my stomach. The stomach that used to hold our baby. The stomach that Blaine was sure to kick me in. I didn't want to wake him up but, I had no choice I had to use the bathroom some kind of bad. I shook him as much as I could with my hand hurting like hell. I knew he was tired but, he jumped right up when he figured out it me shaking him and not someone else.

"Grace, baby you're awake. I know you're hurting and shit but, do you need me to do anything?" He asked.

It was cute to see him so concerned. My face was sore but, I still found the strength to tell him what I needed before I used the bathroom on myself.

"Bathroom," I said slowly and as clear as I could.

"Okay, let me know if anything hurts while I help you. Take

your time. Don't rush anything all we got is time. I'm not leaving your side," he told me.

My heart skipped a beat when he said that. I was expecting him to go in on me for not being able to protect the baby. I was scared that the pregnancy was going to be a bad thing but, it wasn't. The pregnancy did what it was supposed to do bring Gully and I closer together. He patiently waited for me to use the bathroom and was right there to wipe me then helped me back to the bed. I took a relaxing breath once I got back on the bed.

"Thank you," I told him.

"You know none of this is your fault, right? If l had known that he would go through all of this to get to you I would've fucked him up when I saw him in here before. He done fucked up for real. Now he's on borrowed time. I hope you don't feel some type of way about me getting at him."

"He took our baby's life. The way I see it. It's a life for a life. There's no other way to look at it."

He gave me a weird ass look then, hopped up to go out of the door. I didn't understand what was going on until he came back and locked the door

"I know you can't really do too much moving but, hearing you say the shit you just said turned me all the way on. I had to let the nurses know that we were gonna need a few minutes to ourselves. Open ya legs," he demanded.

"Huh?"

"I'm not gonna repeat myself."

"Baby, I just lost the baby we can't do all that. I feel nasty and I know I'm still bleeding. That gross."

"How is it gross baby? You do realize your ass has been out of it for three fucking days. The nurses don't clean you up. I do because they asses might be gay, or some shit you never know. You haven't been bleeding since the day after you got here. So, tell me again what's so fucking gross. You're my damn baby mama and my woman fuck what other people think."

I had to shake my head at him. Only he would think that something like that. I let a tear fall hearing him call me his baby mama. He wiped my tear and kissed me on my forehead.

"Baby listen to me. I know you're hurt because you lost the baby. That doesn't mean you weren't the first woman carrying my seed. If I have my way, you'll be the carrying all my kids. Shit you'll be the one to carry my last name. Now get ya legs open Grace."

"Germain," I whined.

"You heard me. I need to taste you since you can't get this fucking that I want to give you right now. So, I'm willing to compromise."

He flung the sheets off me. I didn't think that he would go through it until I felt his tongue separate my folds. He had me in the most compromising position that I have ever been in. I was turned on by his actions. Not to mention that he was eating me like I was his first meal in days.

"Ohh Germain you're gonna make me yell in here. Everyone's gonna hear me and they'll think you're killing me."

"Fuck them folks I'm not stopping until you make all kinds of noises in here. Stop interrupting me, I'm busy right now."

He went back in with a newfound determination. I know he was doing the most because he wanted me to act up in here. I got tired of fighting to keep my mouth shut.

"Eat your pussy baby. Damn your tongue feels so fucking good. Ohh my goddddd," I yelled.

I could only move so much without hurting but, I was trying to get his head from between my legs. He slapped my thigh letting me know to stop trying to move him. I felt his fingers slid in my hole.

"Stop fighting that nut baby. Give me that shit that I love. I want it now Grace. Wet up my face with your Boss ass," he said as he continued to lick, and finger fuck me.

"Oh shit. Oh shit baby," I called out as I felt the rush of my orgasm take over my body. My orgasm only made him suck on my clit, finger fuck me and move that tornado tongue of his. "Ahhhhhhhhh!" I yelled out. He didn't stop licking until the orgasm had subsided. He looked at me with so much love and passion that I almost came again just from looking at him. He was all in my face licking his lips and shit.

"Taste yourself baby girl," he said before his mouth collapsed on top of mine.

"You're crazy you know that," I said laughing at him when the kiss was done.

"Nah, I just love your ass Grace."

"Germain," I started to say something but, he cut me off.

"Nah, I mean that shit. I love you Grace. I knew when I found out you were pregnant. I mean that shit. You will never have to worry about anyone coming between us. It's Grace and Gully against the world from here on out."

He got up to get a warm rag from the bathroom. He cleaned me up then sat back down beside me like he didn't just suck my soul out of me then tell me he loved me. I drifted off into another deep sleep when I woke up, he was nowhere to be found. My Auntie GiGi and Adrian were in the room with me playing some card game. They were going back and forth because someone was cheating. They didn't even notice me looking at them.

"Y'all are probably cheating each other," I said as clear as I could. They both looked at me then jumped up to give me hugs and kisses.

"My nephew said for us to let you sleep due to the tongue coma he put you in. Don't tell him that we woke you up. I don't have time to be arguing with him," Auntie GiGi said.

"He did not say that."

"Yes, he did," Adrian said laughing.

"Don't you sit over there looking all embarrassed. We all have been there even though you have one up on me by doing it in the hospital. It's on my bucket list though," Auntie GiGi said.

I could only shake my head at her because she could be so embarrassing, and she didn't care about what she said.

"Auntie if you get in the hospital, you're not gonna be well enough to do no freaky stuff in here. Besides you need to have a boyfriend at least to do all that in the first place."

"Don't be all in my business. I ain't walking around with cobwebs I can guarantee you that. Y'all don't know because I don't suck and tell," she said with confidence.

She had us all falling out laughing in the room. She was a mess but, I wouldn't trade her for anything in the world. After not having a mother of my own she was more than an Auntie to me.

"Hold on, wait a minute. Who is this man? Has he met any of the family? Let me find out you over here keeping secrets."

"A woman ain't a woman if she doesn't have secrets," she said laughing.

Sitting here with them helped me feel a little bit better. They always brightened my day.

"Where's Rick? I haven't seen or heard from him since I got here," I asked.

Rick was one of the cousins that I'm close to. I kept expecting to hear from him but, I haven't heard a peep from him.

"Now you know that Rick ain't bringing his ass up here in this hospital besides to check on his daddy. That boy is so damn complicated most of the time. He told me that he didn't want to see you all bruised up and shit. I call bullshit though. His ass is probably with his dad but, can't come to this floor because he swears he's gonna kill the guys who did this to you," Auntie GiGi told me.

I glanced over at Adrian. I didn't want her telling Auntie GiGi who did this. She was known to try to fight anyone. It didn't matter if you were a man or a woman. She would go toe to toe with anybody. Blaine wasn't even worth the energy. Blaine was going to be the sole reason for his own death if he tried to get at me again. Looking at the clock on the wall I wondered what Gully was doing and when he would be coming back. I missed him so much right now. *Lord please bring Gully back in one piece. I don't know what he's doing but, I have a feeling it's something illegal and dangerous.*

ully

I made it to the house in no time. I had to change my clothes and get my mind right for what I was about to do. I had to handle Blaine before I took my ass back to the hospital. The shit had been eating away at me. The problem with niggas like Blaine was that they thought just because they came from wealthy families that they could do whatever they wanted to do. I didn't ask for his address because that's where he was expecting me to be. Instead I was going to his parents' house. If anyone could bring him to me, it would be them. He loved his parents so that meant they were his weak spot. He had no idea what was coming his way but, he would soon find out. My phone rang as I was tying up my black boots. It had been a while since I had to dress in all black. It felt different but, I was on a mission for sure.

"Yo," I answered.

"We outside," Russ said then ended the call.

I walked out of the house making sure to lock the door. When I got to the car Ricky and a guy named Quell was in the car with him.

"You ready for this shit?" Russ asked.

"Hell yeah, Rick where your ass been at all this time. The last time I seen you was when Grace passed out. I thought y'all were tighter than that," I told him.

"I'm barely hanging on with my Pops being in that fucking place. If I would've walked in there seeing her all fucked up like that, I would've went the fuck off. I'll explain that to her when I see her. This nigga has to die tonight. Why the fuck would he do that to her. Just because he ain't want his folks to know he likes getting fucked. None of that has anything to do with Grace."

"Make sure you at least call her. She needs all her folks around her. How's ya pops feeling?"

"He's still out of it. I just want his ass to wake up. I keep telling him that he can't leave me here with Auntie GiGi yet," he said with a short chuckle.

"Get off Auntie GiGi man. She's thorough as fuck and you know it," I said laughing.

"Shit, thoroughly crazy that's what the fuck she is."

"Did y'all forget there's two other motherfuckers in the car with y'all. You two chopping it up like we're not about to go fuck this niggas life up. Plan the family reunion after we get this over with. It's gonna be a long ass night," Russ told us.

I nodded my head because he was right. We needed to have our heads focused on what we had going on. I could talk to him later about Grace. I wanted to be at the hospital with Grace but, I was going to be there when they discharge her. Seeing her cry brought out feelings that I couldn't explain. I hope Blaine is ready for the shit he started.

OOOOO

The house that Blaine's parents lived in was big as hell. It reminded me of one of the houses that we would see on that show, *MTV Cribs*. Too bad it was about to be a murder scene. Just like we knew no one was home right now. Russ kicked the back door in. They were so cut off from the ghetto that they didn't feel the need to get a security system for this big ass house. Once we got in the house, we got everything set up and waited for his parents to arrive.

The front door opened, and they walked in trying to turn the lights on. When they didn't come on, they still hadn't notice Russ, Rick and I sitting in the dining room. We watched as they talked about calling the light company. The husband found a flashlight turned it on then dropped it when he saw the three of us sitting at the table.

"Who the hell are you? Why are you in my house?" The mother asked.

"I'm gonna call the police," the father said.

We were still just looking at them not saying a word. The shit was kind of funny how they were acting. I know if we did some shit like this at a hood niggas house we would be fighting right now. Instead these two were standing here in full panic mode. I took my gun out and sat it in the middle of the table.

"I need you both to be quiet and sit down. As long as you shut the fuck up and do what you're told then you won't be hurt. If you start talking, then all bets are off. I can tell you right now I was raised not to hit a woman but, I will slap the shit out of a stuck up bogouise bitch any day."

They looked at each other then took their seats. You could tell that both of them were nervous as they should be.

"I need you to call your son over here. Tell him whatever bull-shit lie that you want but, get him over here."

"What do you want with Blaine? I'm sure he's not associated with people like you. He's an upstanding citizen. He would never be caught on your side of town," the mother said.

"Dis bitch," Russ said.

"You don't know the half about what your son would do. Just call him so we all can get some clarity tonight."

"If we call him are you going to let us go? How can we be sure that you won't hurt us or him?"

"I guess you can't be sure of shit. Call him," I said.

The mother took the phone out and called the bitch ass nigga. She told him some bullshit about the lights being out and his father needing help to get them back on. He told her that he would be on his way in a few minutes. I already knew that he stayed ten minutes away from his parents, so we weren't going to have long to wait.

"Can you tell me what this is all about?" The father asked.

"Your son has some things to tell you and he can't seem to keep his hands to himself. That's all I'm gonna say for now," I told him.

"I know my son wouldn't hurt a fly. This has to be some type of misunderstanding," the mother said.

"Yeah, a big ass one but you two are the ones that don't understand," Russ told her.

A few minutes later the front door opened and in walked the nigga that was gonna die tonight for sure. When he saw us sitting at the table and the gun in the middle of the table he stopped.

"What … What are y'all doing here?"

"Son, do you know these people?" His mother asked him.

"Yeah motherfucker do you know us?" Rick said.

"Yeah Ma I know them. They are friends of Grace's," he answered. He was still standing in the same spot. His eyes were on me but, it wasn't time for me to talk to his ass right now.

"Why would friends of your fiancée be in our house with a gun?" His father asked.

"Fiancée?" Russ, Rick and I asked together. Quell was standing still being quiet because he didn't know the specifics on the situation going on with Blaine and Grace. He was just here to back us up.

This nigga had lied to his folks. I knew he was holding out that he was gay but, his grown ass was lying on Grace as well. His father looked at our faces and shook his head.

"Son, what's really going on? If these men are here and know Grace, why don't they know that you two are engaged to be married next month?"

Blaine looked at me before turning to his parents.

"Grace and I aren't getting married. We aren't together and haven't been for a while," he said then stopped. I picked up the gun cocked it and pointed it at him.

"Tell them everything and I mean every fucking thing."

"What is he talking about? What else do you have to tell us?" His mom asked.

"I umm… I'm gay. I have been since before I went to college. I didn't want to tell y'all and Grace found out that's why she left me. I've been trying to get her to come over here to act like we were still together. She kept saying no," he said then stopped.

"Tell them how you went to my house and beat her so bad that she lost our baby. Tell them how you know your life is about to end. You took my baby from us so I'm taking you from them. A life for a life sounds about right to me."

"Blaine please tell me you didn't hurt that girl for your own selfish reasons. How could you? We didn't raise you to be that way. Why wouldn't you just tell us that you're gay? Gay isn't as bad as being a murderer. You killed her baby! You deserve everything that you're going to get. I can't believe you."

"You're no son of mine," his father said. He turned and looked at me. "Take his ass out of here. You do what you have to do. You won't have to worry about us saying a damn thing. Just give me enough time to call my lawyer and take him out of the will. I'll just send Martina to handle everything regarding you."

"Oh, shut the hell up we knew that he had some sugar in his tank just like you. You and Lester were more than friends for years thinking that I didn't know. I knew, I just didn't care because I was fucking the mailman every chance I got. So, if you're disowning him then look in the mirror and disown yourself too." The mother said.

I wasn't concerned about the bullshit she was talking. The only thing that stood out to me was the name Martina.

"Martina? You have a sister named Martina?" I asked.

"Yeah, I do," Blaine answered.

He was looking like he was sad as hell to hear that his parents weren't gonna fuck with him anymore. He was gonna die anyway so it didn't matter one way or the other.

"Do you have a recent picture of her?" I asked.

"Yeah," the mom said.

She got up to get a picture. When she handed it to me, I got pissed instantly. I showed it to Russ, and he was shocked to see what I saw.

"Call Martina," I told them.

Hearing the name Martina being connected as Blaine's sister threw me for a loop. I wasn't expecting that by a long shot. Martina said something about me helping her brother when she stopped by the office I never knew she had a brother in the first place. She was playing some kind of game that I wanted no parts of.

"Are you the reason she's been coming to my office and shit?" I asked Blaine.

He was now sitting at the table with the rest of us. He was still looking nervous as hell but, his feelings didn't matter to me. He was gonna meet his fate just as soon as I find out what his sneaky ass sister is up to. Just by looking at them and knowing what Martina looks like they didn't look like they were that closely related.

"Yeah, she said something to me about buying some land because she had something buried there. She asked me if I would put my name on the land instead of hers. I told her yeah because I didn't know what she had there or was going to put there at first," he answered.

"What do you mean at first, do you know what's there or what she's gonna put there?"

The front door opened and there was Martina dressed like she was going to some type of corporate meeting instead of coming to her parents' house.

"What are y'all doing here? What's with the guns? What's going on here?" Martina asked looking around.

"Is this the brother that you wanted me to help?" I asked her.

"Yeah, but you would've been helping me he's only putting his name on the property," she answered.

"What's so special about this piece of land? Why do I need to help you so bad?"

She had been coming to the office and shit, so it had to be something major going on with this land. I watched her as she nervously looked around the room. I was waiting on her answer but, she looked hesitant as hell to even say anything.

"I need to make sure this land doesn't get developed. The only way to do that is to buy it," she said as she shrugged her shoulders.

"What are you hiding on that land? What the hell is buried there?"

She was too adamant about me helping and getting her hands on the land.

"Here comes the bullshit," Russ said shaking his head.

I didn't say anything because I agreed with him. I knew she was coming out of her mouth with some shit that was off the wall. Everyone had eyes on her. She cleared her throat then started biting her lower lip.

"My husband is buried there."

CHAPTER 25

*A*drian

Sitting here with Auntie GiGi and Grace was a well needed laughing therapy session. I had been so down about what happened that I could feel myself slipping into a depression. Russell has been so helpful. He would constantly tell me it wasn't my fault and that I did all that I could do. It helped but I still felt guilty for not bringing my gun with me that night. I wasn't going to leave the house without it from now on. I even had it with me now. Auntie GiGi swore I was being paranoid lately. I didn't say it to anyone but, I've been feeling like someone was following me. I didn't leave the house unless I was coming up here to see Grace. If I left for any other reason Adrian would be with me. I just couldn't shake this feeling though.

"I'm gonna get out of here. I have to go see a man about a horse," Auntie GiGi said laughing.

"A horse? You don't ride horses," I told her.

"Child, I said I was going to see a man about a horse. I didn't say if I was riding the man or the horse, though did I? Pay attention child."

"You are a hot ass mess. I think you need to let us meet this man that you're going to see. He needs to be vetted and inter- rogated by the family," Grace told her.

"I hope you mean your two and Rick when you say family. Your dumb ass uncles can't interrogate shit when they're out here taking care of the community's children. I could tell those motherfuckers that I was Cinderella and they would believe it. I'll set up something with y'all and him those brothers of mine can stay where they are."

She stood up giving both of us a hug and a kiss.

"I can walk out with you. I gotta go to the cafeteria before it closes. I'll be right back Grace," I told her. I walked out with Auntie GiGi.

"When are you and that boy gonna give me some babies to take care of? I'm sure Gully will be shooting up Grace's club again soon."

"Auntie we just got back together. We can't be thinking about having kids right now."

"Why the hell not? You two are in love. Just because y'all were apart physically don't mean shit. Y'all were still connected. When your souls are connected it doesn't matter how long you're apart physically. Trust me on that. Go 'head and bust it wide open for the man," she said smiling then she stuck her tongue out.

I watched Auntie GiGi walk out of the building then, I went to the cafeteria. The food in this cafeteria was pretty good compared to other hospitals. It was seasoned and never too dry. I knew they had to have somebody's Big Mama in the kitchen cooking. I got in the line when a chic came standing next to me. She was standing a little too close for me.

"You're a little close don't you think," I said to her.

She didn't say anything but, she backed up. I paid for the food and left the cafeteria. I was almost to the elevator when I heard someone call my name. When I turned around it was the chic that was standing next to me. I couldn't see her face because she had a hood on. The elevator dinged then I stepped into it when it opened up. I felt a push when I turned around, I saw who this chic really was.

"Caretha! What the fuck are you doing here?"

"I know you didn't think I was gonna let you take Russ and ride off into the sunset. Your young ass just had to come back and fuck everything up for me. Since you fucked up my world then its only right I fuck up yours," she said as she hit the red stop button.

"You stupid bitch. I didn't fuck up anything. According to Russ you two were just in the middle of a fuckship," I told her.

"If it was a fuckship it wouldn't have lasted this long. Your ass didn't hesitate when you left town after I left your mama's house that day. You didn't even call to tell him anything. You just ran like the little girl you were. The night he found out you were gone I fucked him in any position he wanted. When the sun rose the next day, I was back with him again doing things to make him forget all about the fast ass high school girl. You were just to pass the time," Caretha told me.

"I may have been young back then but, it's funny how you did all you could for us to be apart and yet here we are, back together. I was gone all that time but, you and your vintage pussy wasn't enough to make him change your last name. You must be really proud of yourself to be a permanent pussy for all these years. You probably don't even have a key to any of his houses. Damn I haven't even been back in contact with him for six months yet and I have keys to a whole fucking house."

"A house? Russ didn't get you a house you're fucking lying!" She yelled.

I held the keys out in front of her shaking them. She didn't like that much because she knocked the keys out of my hand. I pushed her into the walls of the elevator. We were in the elevator tussling. Here I was again in a fucked up situation and my gun was in the fucking hospital room.

To be continued

www.ingramcontent.com/pod-product-compliance
Lightning Source LLC
Chambersburg PA
CBHW071953150726
47999CB00001B/426